REVENGE OF A GHOST

Mike Simmons

Email: papergirders@gmail.com
www.papergirderspublishing.com

PROOF READING AND EDITING BY
FRAN THORNE

ARTWORK AND TYPESETTING BY
MILLY THOMAS

ISBN 9798292072348

British Library Cataloguing in publication Data
A catalogue record for this book is available from the British Library

*Dedicated to all my friends at the Bear Hotel in Devizes
where most of this book was written.*

CHAPTER ONE

The Scoop

There was tension in the air; it was always the same on deadline day. Sitting at a small desk in the corner of the noisy editorial office of the Sparkbrook Gazette, the reporter Roy Coombs drank strong coffee from a stained mug. Looking around the room at the young, fresh-faced, eager reporters bashing out their latest copy, he wondered how many of them would still be sitting there in twenty years' time; lab rats on a never ending treadmill to nowhere. Like him as a young man, they all saw this job as a launch pad to bigger and better things with dreams of that one big scoop in a national newspaper that would make their journalistic career, or even lead to a job on television or radio.

When he was young and ambitious he aspired to working as an investigative journalist at one of the red top nationals in Fleet Street, London. But he never made it. A friend, who was a sub editor at the News of The World, had once told him that he was too decent a man to work amongst those ruthless bloody vultures in the press room.

Now in his early sixties, twice divorced and suffering the effects of too much booze and cigarettes, Roy Coombs had beavered away in the local press for years. His meat and drink had been a life of reporting on minor cases in the Magistrate's and County Courts, Parish Council meetings and the occasional local sex scandal normally involving a vicar or teacher, most of whom were falsely accused.

He had just finished writing up some mind numbing local story about a woman whose pet Chihuahua had been run down in the High Street by a

1

drunken pensioner on a mobility scooter. After handing it to the sub editor he checked the clock on the wall. It indicated that 'the sun was over the yard arm.' So, much in need of a stiff drink and a smoke, he turned off his laptop, took his jacket from the back of the chair and left the noise of the editorial office behind him.

On his way down the stairs, he met one of the admin assistants. She was always flirting with the young male reporters

She winked. 'Naughty man Roy, you shouldn't cross on the stairs. It'll bring you bad luck.'

He chuckled. 'As if I care.'

On the pavement outside he lit a cigarette then walked along Sparkbrook High Street to his local pub, 'The Artichoke.' It was a bit of a dive but sold decent cheap beer and the landlady was a bit of a looker. Not that he was going up that road again. The last two wives had cleaned him out. At least there were no children to worry about, although sometimes he regretted that.

Amongst others the pub also attracted the type of clientele who, for a small fee, often gave up 'things of interest' to the local press. Normally it was small morsels of local tittle tattle. He had just sat down to enjoy a pint of bitter and a pork pie when a thin faced man known locally as the Weasel sidled up beside him. Instantly Roy could smell the body odour, which did nothing for his appetite. He sighed as the Weasel sat down.

'Well, what have you got for me this time?' asked Roy, with little enthusiasm.

The Weasel grinned exposing his nicotine stained teeth. Leaning across the table he said quietly, 'This could be a big one Mr. Coombs, a real big one.'

Roy took a sip of his beer and replied cynically, 'Oh right, let me guess; the Mayor's been caught in the public toilet with his pants down.' This wouldn't have surprised him as there had already been rumours around the town hall.

The Weasel laughed loudly which provoked a rasping wheeze from deep inside his lungs. 'You're a funny man Mr. Coombs, a funny man. No it's better than that.' He looked around the bar suspiciously, before pushing a piece of paper across the table.

Roy read it carefully. 'Where did you get this information from?'

The Weasel shrugged and tapped his nose. 'You know me Mr. Coombs, 'ear to the ground.'

'If this is true then it's dangerous stuff.'

'So, 'ow much is it worth then?'

Roy folded the piece of paper and put it in his pocket. 'I need to check some things out, but if it's Kosher then I'll see you right. But in the meantime I wouldn't mention this to anyone else; that's if you value your kneecaps. I'll be in touch.'

He stood up and pushed the half-eaten pork pie across the table. 'Here, have some lunch on me.'

ONE YEAR LATER

Peggy, Tim's partner, shrieked in horror. 'You mean murdered?'

Tim shrugged. 'The officer was very guarded; only saying that the police concurred with the scientific evidence that it was highly possible Roy Coombs could have been deliberately targeted by persons unknown. It was all a bit surreal really. The forensic expert said that following extensive examination of the boat, there was compelling evidence to suggest the explosion hadn't been caused by a gas leak but by a detonating device.'

Shocked, Peggy shook her head in disbelief. 'Good Lord! What? A bomb?'

'I don't know,' replied Tim. 'But it certainly seems that way. And why was a detective from the West Midlands Serious Crime Squad even there? All he would say was that the victim was known to them as part of an ongoing case. It's all very strange.'

'Why would anybody want to kill him?' Peggy wondered out loud.

Tim shrugged. 'Who knows, something in his past maybe?'

He flopped down wearily on the sofa and removed the tie Peggy had nagged him to wear. The previous evening, she had cleaned and pressed his brown jacket and trousers. He would otherwise have gone wearing his customary donkey jacket, jeans, and spotted red neck scarf.

Tim was always glad to return home to the peace and quiet of the cottage by the lock gates on the canal. He had lived here since childhood, as had his father, grandfather, and great grandfather before him. He was the last of a generation of boatmen and lock keepers. It was only after his friend Peggy moved in permanently that the cottage acquired a cosiness in addition to its idyllic position by the side of the canal.

Earlier that day he had attended the inquest into the death of Roy Coombs the previous year, when the narrowboat he lived on had mysteriously exploded in Harry Martin's marina. The Melbury Coroner's Court stood adjacent to the mortuary in a small side street off the Market Square. It was an old Victorian red brick building and the heavy dark furniture smelled of recently applied polish. Tim had sat at the rear of a row of pew-like wooden benches. In front of him were, Tim supposed, family members and friends of the deceased. To their left, sitting on separate seats, were the expert witnesses all of whom had given their evidence.

Amongst these there were three accounts, one given by the forensic expert and another by a detective chief inspector; not the local officer who had attended the scene, but one from the West Midland Serious Crime Squad.

It was their evidence, and that of a pathologist which stunned the court and led to the coroner delivering an open verdict. When questioned the forensic investigator had said an ion mobility spectrometer had identified explosive residue around the blast site. The pathologist had told the court that DNA had been taken from the badly burned body, but police had been unable to identify a match.

Peggy and Tim sat in silence for a while, each remembering the events of that dramatic day. It had been like any other day. Tim and Harry Martin, the marina owner, had been talking in the office. The boys, Zed and Dwain, were sitting quietly checking messages on their phones. Then like a sudden roll of thunder, the thud. Windows and doors shook. Swans and geese floating lazily on the surface took to the air in startled flight. Across the marina, angry orange flames and plumes of inky black smoke poured from a moored narrowboat. Later, in a search of the burned out hull, the fire service had discovered the remains of the resident Roy Coombs, who had perished within the inferno.

As the acrid smoke had spread like a cloud across the rippling waters, Harry Martin, his face ashen, had collapsed into a chair; each breath harder to find as a vice like pain crushed his chest. The paramedics, saviours in green, administered kindness, oxygen, and morphine. Tim, Zed and Dwain, battered and blackened after quickly moving adjacent boats away from the fire, watched anxiously as Harry, now with a flush of pink to his cheeks was lifted into the waiting ambulance.

For Zed and Dwain, now moving towards adulthood it was the first of two reminders that all in life's garden is not always rosy. They would become aware of this during the following days as the stench of the burning boat lingered in their nostrils and clung to their clothes like clay.

THE PRESENT DAY

It was four o'clock in the afternoon. As usual Lady Barrington Gore parked her ageing green Range Rover in Tiddledurn High Street. This was a routine she followed every day whilst waiting for her two teenage children, Phoebe and George, to arrive on the school bus from Melbury. She listened to Classic FM on the car radio, sucked a boiled sweet and flicked through a woman's magazine. These days she tried never to think about the cellar in the Manor House with the bricked up wall where Zed, Dwain, George and Phoebe had once discovered the skull with the hollowed out eyes.

The bus drove slowly around the corner and halted outside the post office. There was a hissing noise as the air brake was applied and the double doors at the front opened with a slam. Seconds later noisy, uniformed youngsters poured out onto the pavement, dispersing in all different directions. As usual Lady Barrington Gore waited a few minutes for her twins, whilst teenage love played out those final moments of parting, albeit for only twelve hours.

Now at Melbury college, Dwain and Zed finished their day earlier and were always at Tiddledurn to meet the school bus. Phoebe and Dwain would hold hands and embrace; the kiss now longer than a peck, though not quite French. Their passing school friends would make adolescent remarks to them. Dwain would remove his hand from Phoebe's back just long enough to make a V sign to them. For Zed and George there was no such public demonstration of affection. Only the most avid observer would have noticed their eyes meet and a fist bump where the knuckles touched for longer than usual.

Dwain was like a brother to Zed and, even though the same age, was very protective towards him. He had told them both to 'come out,' and sod what other people thought. George, being the more outgoing of the two, was ready to follow this 'advice' from his friend. Zed though, being more sensitive, was horrified that people should find out he was gay. Not that he was even sure if he was, though he did have feelings for George that were beyond just friendship. George had said that he had known he was different from an early age. Zed though had had no such realisation until meeting George, and even now could not describe the feelings. To him, it just seemed normal.

The first floor flat above Strout's butcher's shop in Tiddledurn High Street was compact and warm. It was now home to Betty, Zed's gran. Prior to that and following the fire which had gutted her narrowboat, Peggy had lived there for a short time. Zed and Dwain always stopped in to see her on their way home from college. The portly Mr. Strout waved to them from behind the shop window, his rugged face as red as the blood stains on his apron.

Zed knocked. A few minutes later Betty opened the door. Seeing her, Mr. Strout winked and raised his straw boater. Quickly she hurried the boys inside and closed the door. Zed laughed. 'He's still after yer body Gran.'

She shook her head. 'Lecherous old fool. He's got no chance, and anyway he smells of meat.' The boys laughed and ran upstairs.

In the sitting room Betty put a plate of jam doughnuts and glasses of cola on the table. They were quickly demolished. Betty laughed. 'Didn't you have any lunch at college?'

Zed grinned. 'That was three hours ago Gran, we're growing lads.'

The transport café in Sparkbrook Main Street, an inner city area south east of Birmingham centre, was a world away from the sleepy West Country village of

Tiddledurn and its neighbouring market town of Melbury. They sat at a square table covered with a ripped plastic cloth. The interior was shabby and worn, with an odour of fried food lingering in the air. Three people, related by circumstance, brooded sullenly over mugs of milky tea. Occasionally they glanced about them, keeping their voices low and guarded.

Each of them had now enjoyed a period of untroubled trading in their respective businesses; the publican, the Indian restaurant owner, and the book maker. There had been other victims in the area, but these three men had bravely spoken in confidence to the reporter Roy Coombs from the Gazette, a local newspaper. He had contacted them to check the authenticity of a story he had obtained from his source, the Weasel.

After some hesitation they had agreed to trust him and reveal the extent of the protection racket they were being subjected to. When he asked why they had not gone to the police they explained that the police were not an option for fear of reprisals and corrupt officers in the pockets of local criminals. Now they faced the dreaded realisation that their past tormentors, Duncan Hicks and Sahil Ali, were soon to be released from Winson Green prison.

That they were ever convicted in the first place was down to the damming evidence gathered over months by Roy Coombs.

CHAPTER TWO

Sweet as a Nut

Tim sat with his feet up on the desk in the small marina office, a large mug of strong tea beside him. Unlike the administrative chaos in which the owner Harry Martin had dwelt, there was now order and tidiness amongst the shelves and filing cabinets. Peggy had seen to that. She would not arrive until later that morning, hence Tim's boots on the desk.

Neither he nor Peggy regretted the day when, following his heart attack, Harry Martin had asked them to take on the management of the marina. Although Tim was sad to see the departure of the two community boats, Odin and Thor, operating them and working self employed as a marine engineer was becoming more difficult for him. As Peggy often reminded him, neither of them was getting any younger.

He stood up from the chair, stretched and walked to the open door. It had just turned nine o'clock and a fine spring morning was spreading across the marina. On the far side he could see two figures in overalls standing on the stern of one of the hire boats. Zed and Dwain had been sent to fit a new exhaust pipe. Tim was a practical man, good with his hands and always happy to work on his own. Now though he looked proudly at his two young protégés.

They reminded him of his young self, all those years ago, under the tuition of his own father and grandfather. The two seventeen year old teenagers were like sons to Tim and Peggy. They had not had the easiest of starts in life, particularly Zed; the flat he shared with his gran in a rundown part of South London destroyed in an arson attack and his young mother dying from a drug overdose. Tim and Peggy were determined to give them a chance to succeed in life and Betty, Zed's gran, some peace and quiet in her latter years.

Since leaving school two years ago Zed and Dwain had been undertaking a marine engineering course at Melbury College. On day release once a week they did work experience with Tim at Harry Martin's marina, and of course were on hand to help out at weekends. Thanks to Harry Martin they received a generous hourly rate for their efforts, although were always broke when the following weekend came around.

There was a loud clang as the adjustable spanner dropped from Zed's slippery hand into the bilges beneath the engine. He swore loudly. Dwain laughed. It had taken them both two hours to fit a new exhaust pipe and they had just finished tightening the last of the nuts. Zed clambered down the small space to retrieve the spanner. 'There's a lot of water in here,' he called.
Dwain shrugged. 'Probably needs a replacement bilge pump. I'll let Tim know.' While Zed wiped his oily and wet hands on his overalls, Dwain replaced the engine cover then turned the ignition key. As the engine fired up they listened for rattling or signs of any escaping smoke. There was none.

'Sweet as a nut. Job done,' said Zed.

The taxi drew slowly through the marina gates and stopped in front of the office. Hearing the car's engine outside, Tim quickly removed his feet from the desk and went to meet Peggy. She stepped from the car wearing a long flowery dress with a homemade knitted floppy red hat. Zed and Dwain called this her hippy look.

The boat's engine spluttered to a halt as Dwain turned off the ignition. For safe keeping he dropped the key into the pocket of his overalls, although it did have a cork ball attached just in case it fell into the water. Zed carried the small metal toolkit they had used for the job. The wooden finger pontoon joined onto a broader jetty which led to the access road. There were a number of empty moorings, which was usual for this time of year when boaters were out cruising on the canal.

At the far side of the marina, where tall sycamore trees bordered the edge and a narrow bridge crossed the entrance, the boys walked past the site of the explosion which had killed the newspaper reporter Roy Coombs. Although some weeks later the boat had been craned out and removed, the charred and blackened pontoons still remained.

Neither Peggy nor Tim had revealed to Zed and Dwain the shocking evidence given at the coroner's inquest. As far as the boys were concerned it had been an unfortunate accident, most likely caused by a gas leak.

When they arrived at the office Peggy had made some tea and put a plate of biscuits on the desk. Seeing them in the doorway Tim asked, 'How did it go then?'

Again, Zed repeated, 'Sweet as a nut. Job done.'

Tim smiled. 'Good, then you're ready for the next task?'

Before they could reply Peggy said, 'Good grief man, give them a break.'

Dwain laughed. 'He works us to death.'

Tim took a mouthful of tea and stroked his now greying, droopy moustache. 'And the bad news lads, is you've another fifty years of it.'

He opened his hands showing his coarsened and hardened palms. 'That's what hard graft does.'

Peggy shook her head. 'Listen to him. Anyone would think he had spent a lifetime down the coal mines.'

Tim retorted, 'Show me your hands then.'

Peggy clenched her fist. 'I'll show you this in a minute.'

The boys opened two cans of cola and laughed. Over the years they had grown used to this playful banter between them.

In the café at Sparkbrook, the bookie, Peter Baxter, addressed the other two men around the table.
'So, what are we going to do then?'
Incredulously they looked at him. 'What the hell can we do?' asked Amit Thakur, owner of 'The Imperial Spice' restaurant.
Peter replied angrily, 'Well, we can't just wait until they or their gang pick us off, can we?'
'They've got no proof it was us who spoke to the journalist,' said Gerry Carter, the publican.
Peter Baxter shrugged. 'Yeah, but we can't take that chance, and even if they don't, who's to say they won't return to their old antics of fleecing us dry again.'
'But surely this time the police would intervene,' said Amit Thakur.
Peter Baxter laughed. 'Don't kid yourself mate; half of the old bill are still in their pockets.'
Gerry Carter stood up. 'I'll get some more teas in.'
The café proprietor, a grubby, obese man in an equally dirty apron looked miffed that the three men had been there for over an hour and only ordered teas.
'You eating?' he asked abruptly.
Fearing for his health, Gerry Carter politely declined the request.
As he sat back down at the table, Peter Baxter suddenly announced, 'There is another file.'
'A file on what?' asked Amit.
Looking nervously around the café he replied, 'Further evidence of their and their gang's criminal activities.'
'How do you know this?' asked Gerry Carter, shocked.

'The journalist, Roy Coombs, he told me after they were convicted. He reckons there's enough evidence in it to put them away again for even longer.'

The other two men spoke not a word as they digested the significance of this revelation.

'So, where is this file?' asked Amit.

Peter shrugged. 'In a safe place with Roy Coombs I imagine.'

'I heard he'd been given police protection after compiling the evidence against them,' said Gerry Carter. 'He could be living anywhere, even abroad.'

Peter drained the last of his tea from the mug. 'That's right, so we had better find him before those two bastards are released from prison. And let's hope they don't know about the file.'

Weary from his journey, Smokey Joe sat down and offloaded his heavy rucksack. Taking from it his old army greatcoat he laid it on the ground, then removed his wide brimmed hat with pheasant's feather. The summer sun was slowly sinking on the horizon and the calm waves crawled gently onto the pebbled beach at West Bay in Dorset. A scattering of late evening walkers, some with over inquisitive dogs, strolled slowly along beneath the towering sandstone cliffs.

He was nearing the end of his journey around the West Country, which had started two years earlier in the village of Tiddledurn and taken him as far as Land's End, where he had spent a month camped on the westernmost peninsula of England. Although as his old, departed mate Driftwood used to say, 'For a man of the road, there is no beginning or end, just another unexplored pathway and open road to roam.' How he missed the old devil and wished he was here with him now. But Driftwood was pushing his old pram along the tracks of 'Skiddledoor,' the resting place for men of the road.

His hike that morning had started nine hours earlier, twenty miles away in the harbour town of Seaton in Devon, where he had spent a semi comfortable night in a sea front bus shelter. Now he was looking forward to a meal and a good night's sleep; but first a paddle in the sea to sooth his tired and aching feet. He had earmarked a small wood on the outskirts of the village to pitch his tent overnight. Now though the light was fading fast and he was hungry and tired.

Looking around the stretch of Jurassic beach, his eyes settled on a formation of high rocks, well above the waterline. Drying his wet and soothed feet with his socks, he replaced his boots and wandered along the glistening shingle. There was a sandy space between the blue grey sedimentary formation large enough for him to stretch out his frame.

Delving into his rucksack he removed his sleeping bag, a primus stove and nest of billies. In the village he had stopped at a store to pick up three bread rolls and two tins of baked beans with sausages. First though he needed an all-important mug of hot sweet tea. As a curtain of darkness fell across the beach, he turned on his battery powered lamp and lit the primus. Now he was alone, just him and the twinkling celestial sphere overhead. Wonderful.

Smokey wasn't sure why he was heading back, although since leaving the army his friends in Tiddledurn, particularly Tim and Peggy, were the closest thing to family he had. He had slept well under the clear night sky. The breeze had stiffened in the early hours and the swash of waves on the shore had momentarily woken him. Soon though his heavy eyelids had closed and he'd returned once more to a deep and contented slumber.

At first, he thought he was dreaming: a woman's shrill voice, distant in the cold dawn. Shivering, Smokey pulled his greatcoat over the sleeping bag. Then suddenly appearing through the gloom it was upon him; a large, black, slobbering shape, the excited wagging tail an equal for any wind turbine. Smokey Joe yelled as a long, wet tongue assaulted his weathered cheeks.

Seconds later a deeply apologetic woman, warmly clad and clutching a dog lead, arrived on the scene. Now that Smokey had realised he wasn't being attacked by some monster from the deep, he was sitting up and stroking the large head of the black Labrador.

'Sky, come away,' she called. 'I am so sorry, he just took off.'

Smokey laughed. 'Well, I probably do provide a decent scent.'

The embarrassed woman was unsure what to say. It wasn't everyday she discovered a man sleeping rough on the beach.

'You're up and about early,' said Smokey Joe.

'Force of habit I'm afraid. I retired last year after a lifetime of early starts, and it's so peaceful here this time of the morning.'

He grinned. 'Until you find someone like me.'

She laughed. 'Yes, it was a bit of a shock.'

Sky now had his head deep inside the rucksack. Smokey laughed. 'I know what you're after.' Reaching into the bag he pulled out a packet of ginger nut biscuits.

She shook her head in despair. 'Food, that's all that dog thinks about.'

Smokey yawned and stretched, 'Well, I'd better get up. The early worm and all that....'

The woman laughed. 'I think you mean the bird.' She called to Sky. 'Come on you hound, there's no more to eat.'

Reluctantly he jumped over the rock to his waiting mistress.

'It's been nice to meet you,' she said.

Smokey now standing, but still wrapped in his sleeping bag replied, 'Likewise. Have a good walk.'

The woman took a few steps across the pebbles then turned. 'Why don't you join me for breakfast? That's my place over there.'

She pointed to a row of small weather beaten cottages nestling together just beyond the shingle. Before he could answer she called out. 'I'll catch you on the way back.'

Smokey chuckled and said aloud, 'Well Driftwood me old mate, that's an offer you can't refuse.'

He hurriedly packed his lamp, billies, primus stove and sleeping bag into his rucksack then, after putting on his boots, grabbed a towel and went down to the water's edge. Bending down he scooped up two handfuls of the cold salt water and sloshed it across his face and beard. A voice behind him said, 'Are you ready?' She giggled. 'I don't even know your name.'

'Joe,' he said, holding out his hand.

She smiled, 'I'm Beth.'

He collected his rucksack from behind the rocks and they walked across the beach towards the cottage. Sky ran along the shoreline barking at the churning waves.

CHAPTER THREE

Sanctuary

Betty stepped from the shade of her upstairs flat into a bright afternoon. The butcher, Mr. Strout, banged on the shop window and pushing aside a bunch of hanging pork sausages he winked at her. She smiled and quickly scurried across Tiddledurn High Street. Skirting around St. Mark's churchyard she followed the asphalt pathway onto the village green. It was a substantial open space. The far side was bordered by a row of pretty terraced thatched cottages. In the centre, nestling under the shade of a tall and ancient oak tree was the village pond, alongside the children's playground. Around the perimeter were several wooden benches all bearing brass plaques dedicated to village residents now passed away. Betty sat down on one to catch her breath. Although born and bred amongst the hustle and bustle of London she had, over the years, grown to love the peace and quiet of this place. It had provided her with sanctuary after the events which had changed her life and forced her to move from South London. Mainly though she was thankful for the safety and opportunities it had afforded her grandson Zed, and his friend Dwain.

How she wished her own two children Amanda, Zed's mother, and her brother Darren could have been so fortunate. But sadly, despite her best efforts, the malign clutches of the gangs on the Rotherhithe estate in South London had captured their souls. Now her daughter had died prematurely following a lifetime of drug abuse, and her son was a convicted criminal who had served time in prison.

She closed her eyes. In the distance she heard the low thud of leather on willow as cricketers practiced their batting in the nets. A chorus of twittering birdsong came from the branches overhead. Small, excited infants laughed as they fed bread to the waiting ducks. The sun on her face was warm and nourishing. Betty opened her eyes and breathed in deeply.

The beta blockers she had taken before leaving home had done their job, and the pain in her chest had now subsided. Her mind drifted back to that appointment with the local GP, and subsequent examination and CT scan at the Melbury Hospital Cardiac Unit. Neither of which she had told anyone about or intended doing so. She smiled to herself as she recalled sitting in the doctor's office. He was so young, quite dishy really.

Sitting behind an uncluttered desk, he had turned the computer screen towards her. She stared as he explained that these were images of her heart taken from the recent cardiac CT. Then pointing to a criss-cross of fine lines running through the muscular organ said, 'Mrs. Hawkins, you have atherosclerotic narrowing of the epicardial coronary arteries.' She had smiled politely, having not the faintest idea what that meant.

Sympathetically, he said, 'In short, it is manifesting itself as angina pectoris, hence the chest pains and shortage of breath. Left untreated it could lead to a stroke or heart attack.'

The clang of the bell on the church tower struck three. Feeling better she stood up and continued her walk across the green towards Tim and Peggy's cottage by the lock. Ever since they had been managing the marina for Harry Martin, Betty had taken it upon herself to prepare the evening meal for them and the boys. It was the least she could do, and anyway she enjoyed cooking. But above all, apart from the mornings she worked in Jean's shop, it gave her a something to do.

At the far end where the path met the busy main road into Melbury Town and the ice cream van was always parked, she crossed onto the narrow gravel track which led to the front of the cottage. It was an idyllic scene. The sweet, sharp scent of freshly cut grass; borders, once barren and neglected, now thanks to Peggy, a blaze of herbaceous colour. The heavy wooden lock gates nudged gently against each other as water trickled between them. By the entrance leading down to the canal, white and pink petals adorned the apple tree which canopied over the grave of Tim's old Collie dog, Barney.

Betty put her key in the lock of the wooden front door. It opened on to a large sitting room which Peggy had now transformed from the former drab and worn interior, into a warm homely space.

Tim watched from the marina office window as the narrowboat moved slowly away from the service jetty. The steerer waved. Tim shook his head then wiping his hands on an oily rag said, 'Five minutes to six. Why do these people leave it until the last minute to fill up with diesel?'

Peggy laughed and closed the laptop she had been working on. 'They probably do it to annoy you.'

He grunted. 'Well, he's succeeded there.' He went to the desk drawer and took out a bunch of keys. 'I'll start locking up.'

Peggy yawned. 'Good idea. Where are the boys?'

'They're tidying the workshop. I'll call them.'

Now that he was based permanently at the marina, Tim had emptied all of his tools and equipment from his workshop at the cottage and transferred them there. As there was no suitable storage space for them, he had ordered a large secure Portakabin which was sited behind the office. Whilst Tim did not share Peggy's penchant for administrative good order, that did not extend to his tools and machinery. As part of their training and apprenticeship, he was constantly impressing on Zed and Dwain the need to look after and value these expensive items, many of which he had accumulated over the years.

The doors to the green Portakabin were open and the boys were sitting outside on the dry bleached grass. Both had their overalls rolled down to their waste and were speaking on their mobile phones. From their body language Tim had little doubt they were in conversation with Phoebe and George. He left them to it and went inside the workshop.

Zed called out, 'Won't be a minute Tim.'

Tim, Peggy and Betty, had been surprised how long these teenage love affairs had lasted. Although Tim once had an historic antipathy towards the Barrington Gore family, he had warmed to the two offspring, who he now saw a lot of.

Having left school at sixteen, Zed and Dwain were now half way through their two year marine engineering apprenticeship at Melbury College of Further Education. Phoebe and her twin brother George, being more academically inclined, still attended the school sixth form to complete their A levels. After that, and providing they achieved their grades, both were destined for university, no doubt a long distance away from Tiddledurn. The thought of this eventual enforced separation depressed all four of the youngsters. There would though be little dissent. Although the family was now a shadow of its former aristocratic, land-owning self, Lord and Lady Barrington Gore would accept nothing less, and not to any old university either.

Tim busied himself inside the workshop whilst Zed and Dwain finished their calls.

'Well done lads, looks nice and clean. Come on, time to go home.'

He closed the heavy steel doors and secured them with a large padlock. Peggy had closed the office and was waiting next to Tim's old Land Rover.

It was not a long journey through the lanes to the cottage. Zed, who was bouncing about in the back with Dwain, shouted, 'I hope Gran's got something nice for dinner. I'm starving.'

Tim called back, 'You're always starving.'

Zed laughed. 'Well, I'm a growing lad.'

Peggy thought to herself. 'Yes, you are certainly that.' He was almost unrecognizable from the scrawny, ginger-haired, eleven year old boy she had found stowing away on the narrowboat, Kingfisher, seven years ago.

Dwain was first through the cottage door. 'Wow, Gran! That smells good.' He also called Betty, Gran; a mark of respect for a woman who, like Tim, Peggy and Zed had become his second family. His own mother had moved with his sister and her fatherless baby to Catford; still in South London but marginally safer than the blighted neighbourhood of the Rotherhithe housing estate where, like Betty and Zed, they had previously lived. Dwain spoke to them on the phone every week, but they knew he and Zed could never safely return to South London.

Betty emerged from the kitchen wearing a flowery apron. 'Had a good day boys?'

They both kissed her on the cheek.

'What's cooking Gran?' asked Zed.

Peggy smiled. 'Liver and onions, Tim's favorite. Now go and get washed and get those dirty overalls off.'

'Good on you Betty, nothing like a nice bit of offal,' said Tim.

'What's offal?' asked Dwain.

Tim laughed. 'The organs of a butchered animal; same as kidney or tongue.'

Dwain grimaced. 'That's gross man.'

Tim rubbed his stomach. 'Nothing like a nice stuffed heart.'

The boys looked aghast.

'What did you think it was?' asked Peggy.

Zed shrugged. 'Dunno really, just liver. Never heard it called offal before.'

'Well it's ready. Do you still want some?' asked Betty.

'Course,' replied Zed smiling. 'I'm starving.' Tim shook his head in despair.

There is a nakedness to the stretch of canal which meanders past the deserted Muckle Farm. The grass now grows tall where once two narrowboats had hugged the bank below the bridge. One mooring had been occupied for many years by Rose, a mildly eccentric woman considered as such by local people as she dispensed healing herbs gathered from the local woods.

Rose also adopted abandoned teddy bears which she lovingly repaired. She maintained they came alive and danced around the bear tree, now a blackened skeleton of its former self due to a lightning strike.

When Zed and Dwain had first met her they were slightly wary, convinced she was a witch. But advancing years and too many winters on the towpath had proved difficult and she had moved into a soulless sheltered housing complex in Melbury, where at least she was safe and warm.

Rose had wept on the shoulder of her dearest friend, Rocket Ron, as she left her boat for the last time. After all it had been her home since she was a young woman. He too had a tear in his eye and kissed her tenderly on the cheek. There wasn't much to take with her; she had few clothes and possessions. Her beloved collection of abandoned bears was taken from the trunk beneath the table and carefully placed into black plastic sacks. They would have pride of place in her new dwelling.

Ron had eventually persuaded her to dispose of the herbs and storage jars. At first reluctant, she had agreed, accepting that the other residents of the sheltered home, might not appreciate the pungent smell of boiling herbs wafting through the corridors.

Rose had consoled herself that the boat was going to someone she knew and would be well cared for. The buyer had been Tim, who had given her a more than generous price for the aged vessel. The day after Rose had left Tim had moved the boat from the mooring alongside Muckle Farm, through the lock, to its new home in front of Turtle Two. Its new resident would be Dwain.

The second boat had belonged to Rocket Ron. He too lived alone apart from his two pet ferrets, Frankie and Freddie, and had feelings for Rose which he could never realise; he was devastated when she announced her intention to move off the boat. After all their time together the thought of remaining there alone haunted him to the core. This hadn't been lost on his good friends Tim and Peggy.

There had once been a third boat, albeit moored further along; Peggy's boat, Turtle. One awful winter's night, Turtle had been consumed by fire. It was due to the bravery of Rocket Ron who had pulled her out, that she escaped the inferno with her life. Peggy lost everything and moved into the small flat above Strout's butcher's shop in Tiddledurn, now occupied by Zed's gran, Betty.

Now Rocket Ron's boat is moored in the space once reserved for Tim's two seventy foot community boats, Odin and Thor, and a short walk from the cottage by the lock. Frankie and Freddie are happy as they have new territory to explore.

After they had finished dinner that evening, Tim sat on the bench outside the cottage gazing lazily across the canal to the fields beyond. Zed and Dwain sat on the balance beams staring hypnotically at the screens on their phones while Peggy and Betty caught up with the latest depressing episode of 'Eastenders' on the television. Gently the light outside started to fade and the deep verdant green morphed to a greyscale landscape.

After their programme had finished Peggy came out with a mug of tea for Tim. 'Do you boys want a drink before you go back to the boats?'

They both replied in unison, 'Please Peg.'

Although eating and having their washing done there, neither boy had slept overnight at the cottage for a long time.

Eventually, following the destruction of Turtle and after much searching around the country, Peggy had acquired another vessel from a boatyard in Watford. It was aptly re-named Turtle Two. Her intention being to live afloat again, something she had done for many years beforehand. This plan though had been abandoned after Zed and Dwain, in danger of reprisals from the gangs on the Rotherhithe estate had been forced to leave London, moving permanently to live at the cottage in Tiddledurn.

Now her good friend Tim, a lifelong bachelor, had many skills but looking after two teenage boys in a domestic setting was not one of them. So, Peggy had agreed to move in with Tim at the cottage. There were though only two bedrooms, of which he had one. Before Tim had any amorous ideas, it was made clear she would be occupying the other. The boys, then in their early teens, couldn't be expected to sleep on the sofas, so it was decided to give them their own space on Turtle Two, now moored close by, even though it meant them sharing a double bed. But that was then. Now they had the luxury of a boat each.

It was dark when Zed and Dwain left the cottage to walk back to the boats. Tim had given Betty a lift home to her flat in Tiddledurn High Street. Peggy welcomed this quiet interlude. Taking out her knitting, she was determined to provide Tim with a warm replacement winter jumper. His current one had more holes than Emmental cheese, though she knew it would be a struggle getting him to discard it.

There was something else troubling her. For some time now, she had noticed Betty's increasing difficulty with breathing, and resolved to raise it with her when they were next alone.

CHAPTER FOUR

The Search Begins

DCI Collins, the senior officer of the Serious Crime Squad at Sparkbrook Police Station, was sympathetic. Looking across a cluttered desk at the bookmaker, Peter Baxter, he said, 'Mr. Baxter, after what those villains put you and the others through, I can understand your plight.' He shook his head. 'But unless they commit another crime when they come out of prison, there is nothing more we can do. As far as the law is concerned, they've done their time.'

This was the official response Peter Baxter had expected from the police, and it was the only one the DCI intended giving him. Frustrated, he felt like saying, 'You know bloody well they will re-offend. It's in their DNA.' But instead, he asked, 'Can you give me any information on the location of Roy Coombs, the journalist who gave evidence at the trial? I gather he no longer works for the local press.'

DCI Collins looked uncomfortable at this unexpected request. 'Why do you want to speak with him?'

Peter shrugged. 'Oh, there are just some things I'd like to follow up with him.'

The DCI looked suspicious. 'After the trial Roy Coombs was placed on a police protection programme, for his own safety. Duncan Hicks and Sahil Ali associated with some pretty nasty characters who were pissed off when they were sent down. So, as I'm sure you understand, I can't reveal anymore.'

It was quite clear he knew more than he was saying. Feeling frustrated Peter stood up. 'Thank you for your time, Chief Inspector.'

They shook hands. He crossed the room, opened the door and stepped into the hallway. A few steps along, a voice behind him said, 'If I had my way, scumbags like that would rot in prison forever.'

Peter turned and smiled at the detective.

Across the road from the police station was the 'Two Moons' pub. He went in and ordered a pint of Guinness. Finding a table in a quiet corner of the saloon bar he sat down and savoured the hoppy bitterness of the Irish stout. Now he needed to contemplate his next move. There were only a few weeks left to locate Roy Coombs and the file of incriminating evidence which hopefully would lead to further convictions of Duncan Hicks and Sahil Ali.

After Peter Baxter had left the police station DCI Collins took the stairs to the second floor and the office of Detective Superintendent Warren Turner, head of the CID which included the Serious Crime Squad. He knocked and without waiting for a reply went in.

The contrast between the two men could not have been starker. DSU Turner was much younger than the inspector, and as a college graduate had risen quickly through the ranks. This direct entry scheme was resented by many of the old school coppers who often remarked that they were good on theory and hopeless in practice.

Bill Collins was one of these. He had started his policing life pounding the beat in Birmingham City centre. Checking shop doors on cold wet nights, dealing with fights at pub throw out time and the often common domestics where a drunken husband thought it his right to use his wife as a punch bag. Over the years he had earned his spurs and had the scars to prove it.

Unlike the DCI's small office, with packed in-tray, littered plastic coffee cups and an overflowing waste bin, Turner's was more spacious and pristine. There was little sign of any administrative activity anywhere. He would often tap the top of his desk top computer declaring smugly, 'It's all in here.' The DCI, not the most computer literate of people, would smile thinking, 'That's all very well mate, until it crashes.' Which it often did.

DSU Turner's slim frame was clothed in a tailored grey three-piece suit with a patterned silk tie. His hair was closely cropped and he wore black framed designer glasses. Bill Collins was now in his mid-fifties and after twenty-five years of thief catching was nearing retirement; a date that couldn't come too soon for him and his long-suffering wife.

Since shedding a uniform to join the CID twenty years ago, his appearance hadn't changed much, except that his dress was now comprised of either blue or brown trousers and a casual jacket. Due to a fondness for a pint of beer, the buttons had long ago ceased to meet in the middle and his shirts and ties all bore small holes, from dropped cigarette ash. His craggy features and baggy eyes revealed a life time of long irregular hours.

There was little warmth between the two men. Turner regarded the DCI as a dinosaur, and he in turn thought the DSU was a politically correct pen pusher.

Turner asked, 'So how did it go then?'

The DCI sat down. 'The bloke is clearly dreading Hicks and Ali being released. It might be worth monitoring their movements for a few weeks.'

DSU Turner sniffed contemptuously, 'Out of the question, we don't have the resources for that type of surveillance and we can't be seen to harass them or their lawyers will soon be banging on the door.'

The chief inspector smiled. 'Yes, you're right, we don't want that. Any way Peter Baxter is keen to speak to Roy Coombs.'

Smugly, Turner lay back in his chair and smirked 'Now that would be difficult, unless he's a bloody medium. Did you tell him?'

Irritated by his callousness, though confident in the broader game plan Collins shook his head, replying curtly, 'No, I didn't.'

Turner smiled wryly. 'For the best. Just as well it was only reported in the local press down there. Let sleeping dogs lie and all that. The investigation is in the hands of the coroner and the local plods now.' He laughed sarcastically. 'And unless they're catching poachers or drunks it's out of their league. So as far as we are concerned the case is closed.'

Tetchily DCI Collins said, 'Officially maybe, but not morally. He was in a witness protection programme for Christ's sake. His death is down to us. How the hell did they locate him anyway?'

Turner's neck reddened against his crisp white shirt. He shrugged defensively. 'We did all we could Bill. Sometimes these things happen.'

Feigning anger, the DCI stood up. 'Well, they bloody well shouldn't. I was the one who persuaded him to give evidence and now he's dead. We failed him.'

He turned and left the office, dramatically slamming the door behind him. DSU Turner, stunned by his colleague's outburst, fiddled nervously with his cufflink.

On his way back down to the ground floor the DCI stopped at the drinks machine and selected a strong black coffee. Outside the main entrance he took a cigarette from a packet, lit it and inhaled deeply. Then smiling to himself said, 'Chickens and Roost.'

Smokey Joe removed his boots before entering the cosy, seafront cottage at West Bay. He hung his greatcoat and hat with pheasant's feather on a hook behind the door before following Beth along the hallway to the kitchen.

'Do sit down Joe,' she said, beckoning to one of four chairs arranged around a small dining table.

Opening a cupboard, she took out a tin of dog food and some dried biscuits.

'I'd better feed him first, or we'll get no peace.' Sky salivated in anticipation. Smokey looked out of the kitchen window at a small garden with trimmed lawn and neatly tended flower beds. Suddenly Beth threw open the back door, shouting, 'Get away you pesty thing.'

A startled grey squirrel jumped down from the bird table and ran across the grass to the safety of a nearby tree.

'They eat all the bread and nuts,' she said. 'Now my dear, what would you like for breakfast? I have some nice bacon and fresh eggs.'

He smiled, 'Whatever's easiest for you, thanks Beth.'

'Right a cup of tea first, then a fry up.' She chuckled. 'I'll be naughty and join you; be a change from porridge.' Whilst she filled the kettle Smokey asked, 'Have you lived here long?'

'Thirty years. Now there's only me and my neighbour left. The rest of the cottages in the row have been sold as holiday lets. It's so sad that local people can't afford to buy them to live in. Even our fishermen are being forced to move further inland.' She put two mugs of tea on the table and sat down opposite him. Sky had finished his breakfast and had curled up in his bed.

Smokey said, 'Wow, thirty years! That's a long time to live in one place.'

She smiled. 'Yes, it is, though it only seems like yesterday when I arrived with such zest and ambition.' She sighed wistfully. 'Where does the time go?'

Smokey detected a tinge of sadness in her voice. He wanted to ask her more but felt it impolite.

She stood up took a large frying pan from a shelf. 'Right let's get on.' Outside the sea mist was clearing and the warmth was burning the dew from the grass. It would be another nice day.

31

'So, where are you heading for?' she asked.

Smokey finished the last of his tea. 'I'm going to move inland, probably head for Dorchester. Legs willing.'

As the bacon and sausage sizzled in the pan, he found himself salivating like the dog who, as the meaty aroma had permeated his nostrils, had left his bed and taken up position by the table.

'And where is your final destination?'

He thought for a moment, remembering Driftwood's words, 'There is no beginning or end.' Then added, 'I'm going to head back to Tiddledurn. I've got a caravan there, though I dread to think what state it's in after two years.'

He omitted to say anything about the house and land which his uncle, old Mr. Coote, had left him and he had rented to a young couple. He expected her to ask, 'Where's Tiddledurn?'

But instead, she said, 'Dorchester's a nice town. You should try to spend a couple of days there.'

'Yeah, I might do that, though I've got to find somewhere to pitch my tent first.'

After leaving Beth's cottage at West Bay, Smokey had climbed the steep ascent of East Cliff to follow the coastal path. The view across the bay was magnificent, with the bright morning sun reflecting off the neon blue sea. At Burton Bradstock, where the rugged path descends back down to beach level, he stopped to cool his hot feet in the River Bude.

It was past midday when he reached the village of Abbotsbury, roughly halfway on his journey to Dorchester. At the top of a hill, overlooking the ruins of the Benedictine Abbey, was a small churchyard. Needing a rest, he pushed open the wooden gate and went in. A narrow gravel path wound its way between old weathered gravestones, their inscriptions faded with time.

The 14th century square tower of St. Nicholas church pressed heavily against the cloudless sky. A high and narrow rounded arch led to two heavy wooden doors. Smokey twisted the decorative handle. He was surprised it was unlocked. Inside he stood for a moment beneath the high barrel vaulted ceiling, decorated with cherubs and angels. Behind the altar a reredos styled with the text of the Ten Commandments spanned the east wall. There was a musty smell to the cool interior.

He was not a religious man. Any sliver of belief in a higher being had been violently stripped from him during his service time in various theatres of war. He had held the hands of too many young men praying not to die, but they still did. There was though something about the stillness of an ancient church which still moved him. He removed his hat and rucksack and sat down on one of the wooden pews.

After breakfast Beth had prepared him a packed lunch and a flask of tea. Flipping open the rucksack he took out a plastic box containing sandwiches, fruit and chocolate. On top was a folded piece of paper. He opened it.

Hello Joe. It was so nice to meet you. Rarely do I come across such a free thinking spirit. Sadly, today we are constantly herded towards docile conformity. A concept I often warned my students against. As Francis Picabia said, "A free spirit takes liberties even with liberty itself." Take care of yourself and if ever you are down this way again, please call in.
Best wishes Beth and Sky.

Smokey folded the note and put it in his pocket. So, she was a teacher. That made sense. He smiled. Meeting people like her always restored his faith in the milk of human kindness, something he had grown cynical about over the years. Soon tiredness engulfed him. He folded his greatcoat into a pillow and lay down.

CHAPTER FIVE

The Lead

Several days after his fruitless meeting with Detective Chief Inspector Bill Collins, Peter Baxter walked into the offices of the Gazette newspaper in Sparkbrook Main Street. He had to start somewhere, and it might as well be here. The single door entrance beside a charity shop window led into a small, brightly lit lobby. A rack holding recent editions hung from the wall. Opposite there were two signs; one pointing to an adjacent room marked, 'Display and Classified Advertising,' the other pointing upwards indicating the location of the 'Editorial Department.' He climbed the wooden staircase to the landing above.

Immediately opposite and behind a small wooden shelf was a sliding glass hatch and a bell. He pressed down on the black button and waited. A minute or so later it slid open, and the face of a young woman appeared. 'Can I help you?'

Peter Baxter asked, 'Is it possible to see the editor?'

The woman smiled, leaving traces of ruby red lipstick on her white teeth. 'May I ask what it's about?'

He hesitated. 'It's rather confidential I'm afraid.'

Briskly she said, 'I understand. Could I have your name please?'

He told her. She wrote it down on a notepad. 'I'll see if he's free Mr. Baxter. Please take a seat.' The hatch closed and she scuttled away, no doubt thinking he had some juicy story to impart.

There was a small green sofa, water dispenser and round coffee table. He sat down and picked up a magazine, considering how he would frame his conversation. There was no point in going round the houses. He would come straight to the point. The woman soon re-appeared at the hatch.

'Mr. Baxter, the editor can see you in twenty minutes. Can I get you a tea or coffee?'

'Tea would be lovely. Thanks. No sugar.'

He thought of all the years Roy Coombs had worked here as a reporter. Surely someone might have kept in contact with him; and what about his family. Did he have any?

She reappeared at the hatch. 'Here you are. Tea, no sugar.'

He thanked her, taking hold of the white mug with 'The Gazette' printed on the side in red writing. As he took a sip of the hot tea his mobile phone rang. It was his assistant at the betting shop updating him with the runners at the Cheltenham and Newbury races that day. He considered the current odds they were offering then smiled. It could be a profitable day.

The door beside the hatch opened and a middle aged man, his receding hair cut short and wearing red cord trousers with wide patterned braces, beckoned to him. 'Sorry to keep you waiting. Come in, bring your tea.' They passed through a large noisy room with four desks on either side. Each one occupied by a reporter, either talking on the phone or tapping a keyboard. The editor smiled. 'Deadline day. All go.' At the far end was a small office with a large window which overlooked the room. The editor pushed open the door. 'Have a seat.'

He flopped into a high backed swivel chair behind his desk. Picking up a notepad and pen he asked, 'So how can I help?'

Peter Baxter replied, 'I'm trying to locate one of your former journalists, Roy Coombs.'

Twiddling his pen between his fingers the editor looked thoughtfully at his visitor. 'Could I ask why?'

Peter took a business card from his jacket pocket and handed it to him. The editor glanced at it, 'So, you're a bookmaker.'

'I am, and that's the reason I'm searching for Roy Coombs. He's won a substantial amount of money on a bet and hasn't turned up to claim it.'

This was patently untrue, but it avoided a more detailed explanation. The editor looked surprised. 'Blimey, I never had Roy down as a gambling man.' He paused. 'Yes, Roy did work for us for years then he became freelance. He was a damn good reporter, a bit of a loner but a nice guy.' Shaking his head, he sighed. 'If only he'd stuck to reporting on local politics and missing kids.'

'I presume you're referring to the Duncan Hicks and Sahil Ali case?' queried Peter.

The editor nodded. 'Brilliant piece of investigative journalism, but way out of Roy's league and ours too. They were bloody dangerous people.' Again he paused. 'You read about it then?'

The bookie smiled. 'I didn't need to; I was one of their victims.'

The editor was shocked. 'Jesus, sorry mate. That's awful.'

'When did he leave you?'

'Not long after Hicks and Ali were arrested. Both we and Roy started receiving some seriously nasty threats; him for investigating the story and us for publishing it. Anyway, the police were under pressure to get a conviction, so they offered him a protection programme provided he gave evidence. Apart from seeing him at the trial, nobody's heard from him since.'

'Is there any family or a friend he might have confided in?'

The editor thought for a moment. 'Not that I know of. There was a wife once, but they parted years ago. As I said, he was a bit of a loner. He used to spend most of his spare time pottering about on that narrowboat of his.'

'Did he live on it?' asked Baxter.

The editor shrugged. 'No, he used to go down mainly at weekends. His long term plan was to cruise the canal network when he retired.'

'So, where did he live in the week?'

'He used to rent a small flat locally, not far from here.' Then anticipating Peter's next question, he opened his desk drawer and took out an address book. Flicking through it, he said. 'Yeah, here you are Flat A, Number 12 Barton Avenue.'

Peter made a note then asked, 'And do you know where the boat is moored?'

The editor tapped his pen on the desk recalling past conversations he had had with Roy Coombs. 'I know it's on the Kennet and Avon canal, but I don't know where exactly, though he did once tell me it wouldn't take him that long to reach Bath.'

'Why Bath?' asked Peter.

The editor shrugged. 'No idea, good place to visit I suppose. Never been there.' He checked his watch. 'Sorry I'll have to go. Another bloody meeting.' Both men stood up and shook hands.

'Good luck with the search. If you do locate him let me know, will you?'

'I will. Thanks for your time.'

Outside, he took the piece of paper with the address on from his trouser pocket. He knew Barton Avenue, it was at the far end of the High Street. 'Worth a try,' he thought. Even the warm summer glow which had spread across Sparkbrook Main Street did little to hide Peter Baxter's despair at the depressed state of his home town. He had been born here in 1974 and had, over the years witnessed the gradual march of social decline and rising crime, mainly due to drugs. He often thought that there was an air of inevitable decay about the place. Many of the shops were boarded up, and the flats above in a state of despair.

On the corner of Barton Avenue was a sweet shop. He knew it well. It used to be a regular haunt for him and his mates on the way to the nearby junior school. He doubted the same nice people were still running it today. He stood looking along the avenue at the rows of once elegant houses, now a shadow of their former selves and mostly converted into flats. Three wide concrete steps led to the front door of number 12. On the wall were four buttons for flats ABCD. He pressed A. After a couple of minutes, he could hear steps coming along the hallway. Then the door opened. A woman, early forties and clearly pregnant asked, 'Can I help you?'

Peter Baxter held up his hands. 'Don't worry I'm not selling anything.'

She relaxed and smiled. 'I am a friend of Roy Coombs, the person who rented your flat before you. Being in the area today he asked me to check if any post had come for him since he left.' A little white lie, but so what.

With her left hand on her not considerable bump she said, 'As a matter of fact there is, we weren't quite sure what to do with it'. She disappeared inside and re-appeared with several letters in her hand.

'Here you are, that's everything.'

Peter said, 'Oh, I thought there would be more than that.'

'There was, but those which were obviously circulars we threw away.'

Peter took them, thanked her and wished her a good day.

On the way back to his shop was the site of the once magnificent Waldorf Picture House. He remembered with fondness the Saturday morning matinees with his mates, watching westerns and war films. Now it was the double fronted 'Square Peg' pub, owned by a national brewery chain selling cheap beer and food. He checked the time. It was well past midday, so after navigating past a group of pavement smokers he went in. Instantly he recognized many of the punters, who later that day would be betting on the horses in his shop.

He acknowledged with a smile those who were propping up the bar and ordered a Guinness and a three ounce American Burger with chips. Sod the doctor's recent warning about high cholesterol. There was a table next to a large descriptive notice advertising the pub chain's latest seasonal offers. He sat down and laid the eight letters on the table. Three in buff coloured envelopes were clearly bills. Four were advertising circulars, but one in a white envelope was from Barclay's bank. He opened it.

Inside was a letter confirming the terms and conditions of a safe deposit box Roy Coombs had taken at their branch in Sparkbrook. But this was one year ago. 'Did he still have the box and if so, why?' He thought for a moment then disregarded it. Even if it were relevant there was no way the bank would let him access it without written authorisation.

He put the letters into his jacket pocket then took out his phone and googled, Marinas on the Kennet and Avon Canal. It was a long shot, but worth a try. His heart sank though when he saw a map of the canal. It was 87 miles long stretching from Reading to Bath. There was also a list of marinas and their location, 'Christ' he thought, 'it will take all day to ring this lot.'

Alongside the mooring on the canal where Tim's two community boats, Odin and Thor, used to be moored, were the stables. The wooden buildings were now in a state of disrepair. Once, the shire horses which had pulled the working boats used to rest there overnight. Behind it was a large field.

Late one summer's afternoon Zed, Dwain, George and Phoebe had gone there to build a fire. They had passed their new neighbour, Rocket Ron, who was sitting outside his boat. His two ferrets, Frankie and Freddie, were scampering about in the grass. Phoebe always kept a wide berth from the furry creatures, fearing one might attack her. Thick woodland surrounded the field, meaning there was no shortage of fuel for the fire. Dwain, being a bit of a pyromaniac, took full advantage of this, causing his friends to complain that it was too hot to sit by. He had laughed and heaped another log on. As dusk descended and daylight slid silently away they drank from cans of lager and watched hypnotically as the orange flames danced and flickered in the gentle breeze.

Zed said thoughtfully. 'It must have been terrible to be burnt at the stake, like one of those witches.'

Phoebe laughed. 'That's an understatement.'

George added, 'Sometimes they used to pay the executioner to strangle them first.'

Cloaked in a coal blackness, with only the light from the fire, Phoebe lay down and rested her head on Dwain's legs. He stroked her long hair. Zed and George sat together holding hands. The occasional bat swooped around their heads then it was gone. Overhead a blanket of stars stretched to infinity. Then, as casual as if he were offering them a Haribo, George asked, 'Anyone fancy a spliff?'

It took a few moments for this sudden request to sink in before Dwain said, 'What, weed?'

George laughed. 'Yeah, I've got some. It's good stuff.'

Phoebe sat up and glared at her twin brother. 'Where did you get it from?' she demanded, 'It's illegal.'

In no mood for his twin sister's goody, goody rebukes, he replied abruptly,

'Does it matter?' He omitted to say it was a boy in his class who was supplying him. This individual had been previously expelled from his private school for this very offence. His exasperated parents had persuaded

Melbury School to take him into their sixth year so he could finish his A levels. He had soon struck up a friendship with George, who had revealed to him that he had once smoked pot at a party.

Dwain shrugged nonchalantly, 'It's cool Pheebs, everyone at our college smokes it. It's no big deal.'

'So, you want some?' said George.

'Yeah, go on then.' After taking a thinly rolled joint from George, Dwain sat back down next to Phoebe. As he lit it and inhaled, she watched him intently. He laughed. 'Don't worry Pheebs, I'm not going to trip out.' Passing it to her he said, 'Here, try some.'

At first, she shook her head then taking it from him took a small puff and quickly exhaled.

Mockingly, George said, 'You're supposed to take it down sis.'

She grimaced and passed the soggy end back to Dwain. 'It's horrible.'

George turned to Zed. 'Come on dude, try one, it will chill you out.'

Zed wasn't sure, remembering his mother's addiction. Although he knew her demise was due to harder drugs than cannabis. He declined though, saying, 'I'll give it a miss.'

George smiled and kissed his forehead. 'That's cool dude, no prob.'

The fire had settled to a bed of glowing embers. Dwain fetched another log and threw it on. A flurry of red hot sparks flew upwards into the night sky.

On the opposite side of the field a narrow torch beam appeared, growing in brightness as the bearer drew closer. Assuming it could be Tim, George and Dwain quickly stubbed out the joints and put them in their pockets. Suddenly Phoebe screamed and jumped up. Frankie and Freddie had run ahead and sought out her legs to sit on. Rocket Ron's short stubby image appeared like an apparition, framed against the glow of the fire, on his head the woollen hat he wore winter and summer. Realising what had happened to Phoebe, he shouted. 'Get away you bloody rodents.'

'Christ, you scared the shit out of us,' said George.

Ron laughed. 'Sorry about that, Can I join you?'

'Course,' Zed replied. 'The more the merrier.'

He sat down on a log and grinned. 'I recognise that smell.'

Sheepishly Dwain asked, 'What smell?'

He chuckled. 'Don't worry kids, your secret's safe with me. Me and Rose were smoking the stuff before you were born and it was a lot stronger than you've got.'

Shocked, Zed asked, 'Rose smoked weed?'

Ron laughed loudly. 'We were the original seventies towpath hippies. Peace and love and all that.'

Tentatively George asked, 'Would you like one Ron?'

He smiled. 'Why not, son? Bring back happy memories.'

George took one from a small tin and passed it to him.

He laughed. 'You can re-light yours now.' They grinned and took them from their pockets.

Zed asked, 'What was it like on the canals in those days Ron?'

After taking a long drag on the joint, he said, 'They were different days, son. There were still some working boats about then. They were real tough characters those old boating families.' He sighed nostalgically, 'Life just seemed so much simpler and slower. People had time for each other. Now it's a dog eat dog world.' He shook his head. 'I don't envy your generation.'

Frankie and Freddie had fallen asleep at the edge of the fire. Phoebe was dozing against Dwain's shoulder. Zed and George were lying down, George's arm draped around Zed's neck, their young cheeks pressed against each other. Ron smiled. Young love, and although he was happy for them, he couldn't help reflecting on his own blighted love life and lifelong loneliness.

CHAPTER SIX

Located

It was the middle of the afternoon in the 'Square Peg' pub. Peter Baxter had consumed his burger and chips without the slightest pang of guilt. He glanced around the busy, spacious bar, many of the tables still not cleared from the last customer's meals. A flat screen television attached to the wall seemed to be permanently tuned to BBC rolling news. Maybe a permanent diet of doom and gloom was designed to make people consume more alcohol. The hardened drinkers and benefit malingerers who had been there since opening time were getting louder by the minute. Time to go. He checked his phone for text messages, then his watch. He had lingered long enough. At the betting shop the punters would soon be gathering to watch the days racing and would be eager to part with their hard earned cash. This was always music to a bookie's ears.

That evening after the elated winners and depressed losers had drifted away from his betting shop, Peter went into his small back office. Sitting at his desk he rang the first marina on the list at Frouds Bridge, Aldermaston. They were helpful but said no such person had ever moored with them. He tried the next, Newbury boat company, the same reply. The clock on the wall showed twenty minutes past five. He thought there was no point in trying any more, they would all be closing for the night.

  The following morning Peter arrived at the shop early. Normally his assistant would open and close the premises. Standing at the front door he momentarily panicked when he forgot the security code for the alarm. Fortunately, he had it saved in his phone. As he pushed open the door a high pitched intermittent wail came from the device above him. Quickly he ran inside and entered the four numbers into the wall mounted box. Thankfully the alarm ceased.

In the broom cupboard sized kitchen he made a mug of strong tea then went into his office. Sitting at his desk he removed from the drawer the list of marinas that he had taken from the Kennet and Avon website. He was not particularly relishing the next two boring hours as he trawled through them. He was about to dial the next one on the list when he suddenly remembered the recent conversation at the Sparkbrook Gazette. He punched the desk. 'Of course,' he said aloud. 'Roy Coombs had told the editor that he was within easy reach of Bath.' Again, he checked the list. There were only three marinas within easy cruising to Bath. It had to be one of them.

That evening he rang Gerry Carter and Amit Thakur arranging to meet them the following morning at the café in Main Street. The three men arrived at eleven o'clock, settled themselves at a table in the corner and mused over mugs of milky tea. Their position afforded them a view of the other customers, mainly builders and bus drivers from the local depot. Amit Thakur, a gourmet of Indian food, shuddered as he watched two large men tuck into a huge greasy fried breakfast.

'We're in business,' announced Peter Baxter enthusiastically.
'I've located Roy Coombs. Now all we have to do is persuade him to give up the file.'
Gerry Carter asked, 'Where is he?'
'At a place called Tiddledurn on the Kennet and Avon canal.'
'So much for anonymity if you found him that quickly.'
Peter shrugged. 'Where there's a will....'

Amit was not convinced of his optimism. 'Why would he raise his head above the parapet again? This time he might get it shot off.'

'Exactly,' retorted Peter. 'That is why we have to convince him to give us the file of evidence he collated.'

'And do what with it?' asked Gerry. 'You said yourself that many of the old Bill at the local nick are in the pockets of Hicks and Ali, or their associates.'

Peter agreed. 'That's right, but I think I've met one who's not.'

'How can you be sure?'

Peter shrugged. 'I can't. He just struck me as an honest copper who wants to see scum like that behind bars for a long time.'

Suddenly Amit stood up saying, 'I need to get out of here, it's making me feel sick.'

The other two men agreed. The intensity of frying food was overwhelming on the senses. The obese owner with the dirty apron scowled as they left. Gerry chuckled. 'He's not long for this world.'

Breathing in gulps of fresh air they stood outside on the pavement.

'Is there anything we can be doing?' asked Amit.

Peter shook his head. 'Not for the moment. Firstly, I need to visit this marina and speak with Roy Coombs.'

Gerry gave a wry smile. 'Let's hope he's pleased to see you.'

Smokey Joe woke with a start as a hand gently shook his shoulder. Having walked from Lyme Bay to Dorchester that morning, he had fallen asleep on a pew in Saint Nicholas Church in Abbotsbury. The voice speaking to him was equally gentle. 'Hello, my friend, I apologise for interrupting your slumber, but I have to lock up now.'

Bleary eyed, Smokey looked up into the kind face of the elderly vicar. 'Oh, I'm sorry, I only popped in for a rest.'

The churchman smiled. 'That's quite aright. God's house welcomes all pilgrims.' Smokey chuckled to himself. He had been called many things over the years, but never a pilgrim.

The vicar sighed. 'Unfortunately, there are those who take advantage of that welcome to steal and vandalise the church. It's very sad, that's why we always lock the doors now at six o'clock.'

Rapidly regaining his senses Smokey proclaimed, 'Oh Christ, is that the time?' Then remembering his hallowed surroundings, he quickly apologised.

The vicar smiled. 'Don't worry. We all take the Lord's name in vain at some time, and you must have needed the sleep. Where are you heading for?'

Smokey Joe explained that he was going home to Tiddledurn and was intending camping on the outskirts of Dorchester for the night.

'Well, it's getting late. You could camp in the field at the back of the church if you like?'

Smokey didn't feel like doing much more walking that day, so he readily accepted the invitation. Picking up his rucksack he followed the vicar outside, waiting whilst he locked the heavy double wooden doors. They walked the narrow gravel path at the side of the ancient church. At the rear, a high hedge separated the churchyard from the small grassed field.

The farthest edge dropped away to a ruined wall. The churchman pointed out that beyond were the remains of the great Abbey of St. Peter with the tithe barn and the monastic pond. To the left of the hedge was a fenced garden, with a gate leading to an old rambling house.

Almost apologetically, the vicar said, 'That's the Manse where I live. Too big really for me and my wife, but it comes with the job.'

Smokey said, 'Looks nice and cosy.'

The vicar laughed. 'The roof leaks like a sieve and its very draughty, but its home.' He pointed to a wooden construction in one corner of the field. 'There's a toilet and drinking water in there.'

Smokey smiled. 'This will do just fine, thank you. You've been very kind.'

The vicar touched him tenderly on the arm. 'Right, I'll leave you to get set up.

God bless. Any problems you know where I am.'

Smokey pitched his tent close to the high hedge. After a meal of savoury rice and sausages, washed down by a can of beer, he took out his phone to plan the following day's hike on Google maps. His destination would be Cranbourne Chase, taking him roughly nine hours.

Sleep overcame him quickly in the onyx black silence of the countryside. His thoughts, often nightmarish and troubled, were now calm and peaceful. His rest though was never deep; this was a hangover from his war zone days. Part of his consciousness, like an alert guard dog, would linger close to the surface, ready to respond to any external intrusion.

At first, he thought it might be the gentle fantasy of a passing dream, but no, the sounds were real and nearby. Now fully awake, he listened for a moment, as amplified by the silence, the whispered voices drifted towards him from the adjoining churchyard. A less balanced individual may have concluded it was the mutterings of the ghostly deceased. Reaching for his phone Smokey checked the time. It was two fifteen in the morning.

Silently he slid from his sleeping bag, crawled out of the tent and pulled on his boots and ex-army greatcoat. As he rounded the end of the hedge, he could make out a faint torch beam close to the porched entrance of the church. Using the larger of the gravestones as cover, he stealthily crossed the churchyard until he was level with the flint stone wall which bordered the road. Fortunately, the quarter moon afforded a sliver of light across God's consecrated acre. Now he could just make out the shape of an open backed van parked alongside the gate.

From the top of the porch a narrow ledge ran the length of the building. Part way along, where the roof sloped towards the square west tower, Smokey again glimpsed the dim torchlight. He muttered to himself, 'The buggers are nicking the lead.'

He thought of the kindness the vicar had shown him and of his despair of the desecration of his beloved church, by pond life like this. Carefully he moved closer to the path, concealing himself behind a chest tomb. Again, the lone figure stumbled before him; the body posture indicating something heavy being carried towards the van. Smokey waited until he had deposited his load and turned to walk back.

The strike, when it came, was as fast and effective as any leopard bearing down upon its prey. Lunging from behind the cover of the tomb, Smokey Joe delivered a powerful punch below the solar plexus, rendering the victim unable to breathe. As the body crumpled to the ground, Smokey turned it over to reveal the face of a man. He placed his thumb and forefinger on the man's throat, pressing down on his windpipe. His eyes rolled, and his legs shook uncontrollably as he fought for oxygen.

Smokey felt a surge of adrenalin. He had dispatched enemy soldiers with this method whilst on special duties in that theatre of war. How easy it would be. Instead, patting his victims sweating cheeks, he smiled.

'This is your lucky day, now you stay there like a good boy, whilst I sort out your mate.'

Walking along the gravel path, he could now see a ladder leaning on the narrow ledge. A voice from thirty feet above, called out quietly.

'Come on, 'urry up. We're nearly done 'ere.'

Gleefully Smokey shouted back, 'You're right there mate,' and with a kick knocked the ladder to the ground. The response was an angry retort. 'What the bloody 'ell's going on?'

Smokey laughed. 'Oi, watch your language mate, remember where you are.'

Safe in the knowledge that the one on the roof wasn't going anywhere, Smokey returned to the other thief, who was still lying where he had left him. Taking out his mobile phone he rang 999.

A police officer knocked on the door of the Manse in the early hours, to inform the vicar that thanks to a bloke camping in the field, they had arrested the men stealing lead from the church roof. Not having the faintest idea what had occurred, the vicar threw his coat on over his pyjamas and rushed next door to the church.

Parked outside the gate was a flatbed van and two police cars, their blue lights still flashing. In the rear of one were two crestfallen men in handcuffs. Smokey Joe, as cool as a cucumber, was sitting on a wooden bench. The vicar sat down beside him. 'What the....? I mean, how.....? Are you alright?'

Smokey smiled and patted his shoulder, 'Don't worry about me Father, one good turn deserves another.'

The vicar chuckled. 'Well, you certainly were heaven sent my son.'

CHAPTER SEVEN

Phoebe's Concern

Dwain and Phoebe lay on the red and white striped duvet in her bedroom at the Manor House. Even though it was summer, a large damp patch stained one corner of the ceiling. Apart from the bed there was an old wardrobe painted blue, a nest of drawers, bookshelves and a desk with a lamp on it. Several school books were scattered across its surface. On the walls there were pictures of Harry Styles and Ed Sheeran, who Phoebe often said reminded her of Zed with his red hair.

It was one of the few upstairs rooms now still in use at the Manor House. It had been home to the land owning Barrington Gore family since the seventeenth century. Now though the house needed costly repair, which the current incumbent, her father Sir Roland, did not have the finances to spare.

Phoebe looked around the large room. 'I hate this place now. It's too hot in the summer and freezing in the winter. I wish Mummy and Daddy would sell it and we could move somewhere smaller.

Dwain asked, 'Is this since the stuff in the cellar two years ago?'

She laughed. 'Well, it certainly didn't help finding those bones down there. Even though Daddy had it bricked up, I still can't go along that passage. It's too scary.'

Dwain rolled over and kissed her nose. 'So, where would you like to live?'

She smiled. 'With you of course, on your cosy little boat.'

'That would be cool Pheebs,' he replied, though they both knew that fantasy would never be realised. It had only been two weeks since Phoebe had argued with her mother over the subject.

'It's not fair, George can stay overnight with Zed, but I can't with Dwain. I'm seventeen years old, not ten.'

Lady Barrington Gore's answer was always the same. 'Precisely my darling, it's because you are seventeen. You're a girl.' She hesitated. 'And, well things can happen. As my mother used to say, - in youth wisdom is but rare.'

This always inflamed the situation even more. On one occasion Phoebe had blurted out in anger, 'And what do you think George and Zed get up to?'

Surprised, Lady Barrington Gore had asked, 'Whatever do you mean dear?'

Realising she had gone too far, and her parents knew nothing of their son's sexuality, Phoebe had fled the room in tears.

Downstairs Milo and Morgan, the two black Labradors, had started to bark. They had heard their mistress coming up the drive. This was Phoebe and Dwain's early warning system.

'It's Mummy back from shopping. Quick. Downstairs.' Although Lady Barrington Gore welcomed Dwain to the house, he was only allowed in Phoebe's bedroom when she was there. By the time her green Range Rover had pulled up outside, Phoebe and Dwain were in the sitting room watching the television.

As she opened the front door, she called out. 'Phoebe, come and help me with the shopping dear.'

Dwain appeared alongside her. Slightly taken aback Lady Barrington Gore said, 'Oh, hello Dwain, I didn't know you were coming over today.'

He smiled. 'Just called in for a chat.'

She gave her daughter a dubious look.

After depositing the shopping bags in the kitchen, Phoebe said, 'We're going out now Mum.'

'Where to?' her mother asked.

Phoebe raised her eyes dismissively. 'Just out.'

'Where are we going?' asked Dwain.

She took his hand, 'Nowhere. I just want to talk to you.'

Leading him around the side of the Manor House, they went along a narrow path which led between two huge rhododendron bushes. It opened onto a small grassed area where a wooden seat stood beside a weed infested pond. They both sat down.

Dwain asked, 'So, what is it?'

'Promise you won't tell anyone else?'

'Of course not.'

'It's George. That weed he's smoking. I'm really concerned where he's getting the money from to buy it. He can be so stupid and gullible sometimes. You saw the other night in the field. He had more than one reefer in that tin.'

Dwain agreed with her. 'Yeah. The stuff's certainly not cheap. What about the allowance your parents give him?'

She laughed. 'No way, that certainly wouldn't cover it, and they'd go mad if they found out.'

'Have you tried talking to him?'

She shook her head. 'He won't listen to me, but he would you. Especially if you said it was unfair on Zed. I mean, in light of what happened to his mum.'

Dwain considered it for a moment. 'Ok, I'll try. But if he tells me to shove off, there's nothing more I can do.'

Phoebe took his face in her hands and planted a kiss on his mouth. 'Oh, thanks D. He won't do that, he respects you.' She had taken to calling him D. It was cool.

The seedy Blue Diamond club, located beneath a railway arch at the rear of New Street Station, was well known and frequented by the inhabitants of the dark underbelly of the City of Birmingham. Jimmy Doyle the owner of the club, a close associate of the gangsters Duncan Hicks and Sahil Ali, took a phone call from Sparkbrook Police

Station. He dragged hard on his cigarette and exhaled as the caller explained there might be a problem. He grunted, 'Like what?'

That afternoon Jimmy tapped a number into his mobile phone. The wing officer at HM Prison Winson Green, who was in the pay of the inmate Duncan Hicks, immediately recognised the brusque voice at the other end.

'Arrange a call with him at six tonight.' The phone went dead.

Later that week, two men arrived at the betting shop in Sparkbrook Main Street. They were unlike the usual punters, more akin to the heavies Hicks and Ali used to send round weekly for the protection money, before being imprisoned.

It was a busy Saturday afternoon as always. Watching the four television screens, excited punters stood noisily cheering on their chosen horse as it thundered around the Newmarket race course. Pushing their way towards the counter the two heavies confronted the assistant, who was standing behind a shatterproof glass screen. They demanded to see Peter Baxter. Nervously he told them he was away on business and wouldn't return for a week. Did they want to leave a message?

The one with the gold cross hanging from his ear drew closer to the screen, 'You wouldn't be fucking with us, would you?' The assistant held his hand up. 'No honestly he's not here.'

'So where is e' then?'

The assistant shook his head. 'I've no idea. He didn't tell us where he was going.'

After eying him suspiciously they left without another word.

The assistant breathed a sigh of relief at their departure, though didn't doubt they would return at some time in the future.

Peter Baxter stepped from his car and stretched. The quaint village of Tiddledurn was certainly a contrast to the sprawling Birmingham metropolis which he had left four hours earlier. The narrow High Street with small personable shops, thatched cottages, and an ancient church; it was like stepping back in time.

He was taken by surprise when several passing people bade him 'a good afternoon.' In Sparkbrook such a gesture would be met with a distrustful glare, or worse. A short way along, between an estate agents and a hair salon, was the Pink Balloon coffee shop. He went in, ordered a latte and sat at one of the small tables. The colourful décor within reflected the name of the establishment. Around him couples sat together chatting over their favourite drink. He missed these moments of intimacy which he used to share with his wife.

The young waitress who brought his coffee and walnut cake was chatty and slightly flirtatious. She chuckled at his unusual broad accent.

'Let me guess.' She paused. 'Liverpool?'

He laughed. 'You're way out. I'm a Brummie, from Birmingham.'

She giggled. 'Oh, silly me.' As she turned to go he asked, 'Do you know the way to Harry Martin's marina?'

'I do. Are you on foot or do you have wheels?'

'Wheels,' he replied.

'Ok, go to the end of the street, turn right onto the Melbury Road. Eventually you will come to a set of crossroads, turn left onto Pig's Lane. That will take you to the marina.'

He grinned. 'That was very precise, thanks.'

She gave him a coquettish glance. 'Anytime.'

He paid the bill and left her a tip. 'Blimey, a few years ago I would have been in there,' he thought.

The short journey from the High Street to the marina took twenty minutes, hampered by a slow moving tractor towing a trailer loaded with bales of hay. Peter laughed to himself. 'You don't see many of these in Sparkbrook.' When he arrived at his destination, the entrance gates were open. He drove through and along a short driveway bordered by neatly trimmed lawns.

A sign stating, 'Visitors Parking' pointed to a wide space beside a brick building. He stopped the engine and stepped out of the car. This was the first time he had been to a marina and he was impressed by the large expanse of water, with the sun glinting off the polished coachwork of the moored narrowboats.

He turned as a woman's voice from behind asked, 'Can I help you?'

Peggy was standing in the doorway of the office. Zed and Dwain, on their day release from college, were with Tim in the workshop. Peter Baxter introduced himself and handed her a business card. She studied it for a moment, then assuming he might be a prospective moorer, invited him into the office.

'Please have a seat.' Sitting down behind the desk, she asked, 'How can I help?'

'I'm trying to contact one of your customers, Roy Coombs. I understand he has a boat moored here,' he explained.

Stunned by this sudden and unexpected request Peggy asked, 'Are you a friend of his?'

Peter Baxter smiled. 'Not exactly.'

Then he repeated the story he had used before, about Roy's big win on the horses and it not being claimed.

Peggy nodded. 'Oh, I see.'

Again, she glanced at the name and Sparkbrook address on the business card and then remembered that it had been an officer from the West Midland Serious Crime Squad who had given evidence at the inquest one year ago when the experts concluded that the explosion could have been caused by a bomb.

As she studied the man sitting before her a shiver ran along her spine and she wondered if this person was really who he said he was. Standing up, she said, 'Would you excuse me for a moment?'

Tim's Portacabin workshop was situated behind the office. Flustered, Peggy ran round and opened the door. Tim, Zed and Dwain were kneeling on the floor surrounded by parts of a diesel engine which they had stripped down. They looked up.

'Good grief woman, you look like you've seen a ghost,' said Tim.

'You need to come quickly. There's a man in the office asking to see Roy Coombs.'

Irritated at being disturbed Tim asked, 'Who is he?'

Peggy shrugged. 'Lord only knows. He says he's a bookie from Birmingham and has some winnings for Roy. Sounds a bit strange to me. Who has ever heard of a bookie chasing someone to pay out?' She paused. 'Obviously, he doesn't know Roy Coombs is dead.'

Tim stood up and wiped his hands on an oily rag. 'I'll be there in a minute, until then make polite conversation.'

'Why is Peggy so spooked about a bloke asking about Roy Coombs?' asked Zed. Tim didn't answer his question, instead saying, 'You two stay here, I won't be long.'

CHAPTER EIGHT

Shock

'This is Tim,' said Peggy.

Peter Baxter stood and introduced himself. Tim pulled up a chair beside the desk. For a few seconds he studied the face of the visitor from Birmingham. He was no physiognomist, but like Peggy a reasonable judge of character. There seemed nothing in this man's pleasant expression or demeanour to suggest any deception.

'Peggy tells me you're looking for Roy Coombs,' said Tim.

'That's right, I am.'

Tim nodded then sympathetically said, 'I'm sorry to tell you but Roy is dead.'

Confirming Tim's assessment of him, Peter was visibly shaken.

'Oh my God, no!'

Realising_this was going to be a long and difficult conversation Peggy said, 'I'll make us a nice cup of tea.'

Peter remained silent for a moment then asked, 'What happened to him?'

'It was one year ago. He died here in an explosion on his boat.'

Peter shook his head. 'That's awful! Poor man.'

Peggy arrived back from the kitchen with three mugs of tea and some biscuits.

'Why are you trying to locate Roy?' asked Tim.

Peter paused. 'I'm afraid it's a long story. There never was a bet or unclaimed money. That's just a ruse I tell people to help locate him.'

Tim laughed. 'It did seem a bit odd, an honest bookie.'

'Don't worry, we've plenty of time,' said Peggy.

Zed and Dwain had grown impatient waiting for Tim to return to the workshop. Leaving the floor scattered with engine parts they closed the door and went to the office. Peter Baxter abruptly ceased his narrative and looked round as the boys came through the door.

'Sorry to disturb,' said Zed, 'we've just come to get some cola from the fridge.'

Peggy smiled. 'Why don't you both take the afternoon off?'

Dwain nodded. 'Sounds good. Shall we hang around here or go home?'

'Up to you lads,' replied Tim, 'but we might be some time.'

After leaving the office, the boys decided to walk back to the cottage along the towpath. 'There's something going on they don't want us to hear,' said Zed.

Dwain agreed. 'It's weird man.'

Leaving the marina by the front gate, they turned off the road and onto a little used footpath thick with underbrush. This short cut would take them across two fields, emerging at the canal edge by Muckle Farm. From here it would be a short walk to the cottage by the lock. A flock of sheep grazed contentedly on the short grass.

'I wonder what they think about all day?' said Zed.

Dwain laughed. 'Eating, that's about it.'

Zed punched him on the arm and ran off, shouting, 'A bit like you then, thick.'

Dwain pursued him calling, 'You're dead when I catch you dude.' He was faster than Zed and soon both boys were rolling about play fighting on the ground. Without any shade from the sun, they soon tired. Both lay on their backs breathing heavily. A plane, high, like a silver arrow, crossed the cloudless blue sky. Zed said, 'I remember standing on the balcony of the flats in London and watching the planes approaching City Airport. They were twin engine A220 Airbuses. I used to imagine which country they had come from. Gran always said we'd go on one, but we never did.'

Dwain shrugged. 'Maybe you will one day, who knows?'

Zed sighed. 'Yeah right.'

Suddenly a deep voice behind them said, 'Alloboyswahtdoing?'

Army Jim's West Country accent was delivered with the rapidity of a machine gun. The two boys looked up at the camouflage clad figure, his creased facial features shaded under a military style combat hat and a long bladed machete hanging loosely from his belt.

Recognising him, Zed said, 'Oh! Hi Jim.' He had always been wary of Army Jim, since first meeting him on the towpath when he was eleven.

Dwain said, 'We thought you were still moored outside Jean's shop.'

'Noanymorerrenow,' grunted Army Jim.

'Why are you in the woods?' asked Zed.

He gave a rare twisted smile, revealing his crooked, nicotine-stained teeth. 'Aftecatchinraabbits.'

The boys stood up. Dwain said, 'Well, good luck. We'd better get going.'

Suddenly Army Jim pulled the machete from his belt and held it out menacingly in front of them. His podgy red fingers clasped tightly around the handle. Surprised, they both jumped back.

'Feelowsharptis,' he said, running his thumb across the cutting edge.

At first, they didn't understand him. Looking anxiously at the long blade, Dwain asked, 'Say again Jim.'

He took a step forward. Again, he repeated, 'Feelowsharptis.'

This time they got it. Smiling nervously, Zed said, 'We'll take your word for it Jim.' Edging past him they quickened their pace into the wooded copse at the edge of the field. Alongside the snaking path, solid tree trunks were pushed together. Thick brambles grew, with fallen branches propped at fractured angles. Dwain checked behind to make sure Army Jim wasn't following them.

'I tell you man, he's a creepy nutter.'

At the far side of the copse a broken stile led onto the towpath. The boys jumped over. Army Jim's moored narrowboat was easily identifiable, being painted in the same livery as his camouflaged attire. In the window a sign read. 'Do not enter. Danger of Death.'

Dwain laughed. 'Told you, he's a bloody sicko.'

A group of narrowboats were dotted alongside the bank. A few of them were what Tim contemptuously called, 'Pikey' boats. He often raged that they stayed too long in one place, made a bloody mess and never had a licence. Looking at the pile of old pallets and discarded beer cans littered outside one, it was hard to disagree with him.

They crossed a bridge to the opposite side of the canal and were soon walking past Coote's Wood, which prompted Zed to say, 'I wonder when Smokey will come back?'

'If he ever does,' replied Dwain. 'He was pretty cut up after Driftwood died.'

'I liked old Driftwood,' said Zed. 'He was a real character. But it's strange what makes people go like that.'

'Like what?'

'Well, become homeless and just wander about the countryside. You know, go off grid.'

Dwain laughed mockingly. 'Off grid, where did you get that from?'

'Oh, shut up. I heard it somewhere. It's what they call it, living off grid.'

Dwain despaired. 'Off grid, my arse. They're drop outs, fed up with life's crap, and who can blame them.'

As they neared the lock by the cottage, they could hear the seepage of water from beneath the heavy wooden gates. A grassy bank led up to the lock chamber.

It was empty. The boys crossed over the balance beam into the garden. Zed put his key in the lock and pushed open the front door. It led directly into the cosy sitting room. A shaft of sunlight came through the window, creating a beam of dusty particles.

Dwain said, 'I'm starving man.'

Zed laughed. 'See, that's what I said. You're always hungry, like a thick sheep.'

Dwain ignored his friend's taunts and headed for the kitchen.

It was not long before they were sitting outside on the wooden bench by_Peggy's rose bushes. Between them a plate of thick cut ham sandwiches, crisps_and a bottle of cola.

'Does it bother you George smoking weed?' asked Dwain.

Finishing a mouthful of food, Zed shrugged. 'After what happened to my mum, course it does. But it's up to him.'

'Don't you ever wonder where he gets the money from? The stuff's not cheap.'

Again, Zed shrugged indifferently. 'I expect he gets a good allowance from his parents.'

Dwain nodded. He knew there was no point in pursuing it with him further. 'Ok it's cool.' That's what he loved about Zed; he saw no wrong in anybody. It was why he felt so protective towards him.

In the marina office Peggy and Tim were visibly shocked as they listened to what Sahil Ali and Duncan Hicks had for years inflicted on Peter Baxter and his fellow businessmen in Sparkbrook.

Peggy asked, 'Why did they only get two years in prison?'

Peter sighed. 'It's good old British justice. They were sentenced to four years, for extortion and threatening behaviour. But apparently you get fifty percent off the tariff these days, spending the remainder of your sentence out on licence.' He shrugged despairingly, 'So they will be out in a few weeks from now, god help us.'

Tim said, 'That's ridiculous. Bloody lowlife. They should throw the key away.'

Peggy observed, 'So, it was really down to Roy Coombs' evidence that they ever got convicted in the first place.'

Peter nodded. 'He was the only one we could trust to tell what was going on. Those bastards were bleeding us dry.'

Tim asked, 'Why didn't you go to the police?'

He laughed. 'Because they couldn't be trusted, many of them were, and still are on their payroll and would have informed Hicks and Ali. Then we would have been toast.'

Peggy shook her head. 'That's terrible.' Then she asked. 'So this file, you said he had?'

'That's right. During Roy's investigation he uncovered a lot more evidence implicating Hicks and Ali and their associates in criminal activity across Birmingham; prostitution, drugs, people trafficking and so on. Apparently there was enough to put them away for a lot longer than two years.'

'But why wasn't that included in the original prosecution?' asked Peggy.

'I did ask Roy that at the time. He said the officer in charge of the case, who he knew and trusted, asked him to hold fire. He was concerned it might muddy the waters on the current charges. Although I got the impression really he was being pressured from higher up; maybe even the local office of the Criminal Prosecution Service. Who knows? Corruption runs deep.'

Tim asked, 'So, you're hoping to get hold of this file, before those two are released from prison.'

Peter nodded. 'It's our only hope.'

'Well surely if he had it with him, it would have been destroyed in the explosion.'

Peter considered that suggestion for a moment. 'I don't think he would have kept it with him. After the trial he knew how vulnerable he was. It would be somewhere safe under lock and key, just in case.'

Tim chuckled. 'Yeah. But without knowing where, you can't get access to it.'

Peter agreed with him then asked, 'Do you have a safe here?'

'We do. But when Harry asked us to take over the marina management, we went through the contents with him. There was nothing unusual in there.'

Peter Baxter nodded. 'Just a thought.'

Peggy asked, 'When you say file, is this in written form or could it be on a memory stick?

Peter shrugged. 'I've no idea. It could be either, or both.' Turning to Tim, he asked, 'Did your DCI say what caused the explosion?'

Tim sighed. 'I was hoping you wouldn't ask that question. I attended the inquest in Melbury. The forensic evidence pointed towards it being some sort of device. In short, it appears he was deliberately targeted.'

The blood suddenly drained from Peter's face. For a moment Tim felt he might pass out. 'Christ, he was murdered then. So those bastards got to him,' he said soulfully.

Tim nodded. 'It would seem so I'm afraid.'

'How did they get into the marina unseen?'

'There's a lot of people coming and going throughout the day. We can't monitor them all.'

'Is there CCTV?'

Tim shook his head. 'Harry never got round to installing it.'

Peggy smiled. 'Our Harry lived in a different time zone, when people were more trusting and could leave their front doors open.'

Tim laughed. 'And the cost of it would have brought him out in a sweat.'

Peggy made some more tea. Tim suggested they went outside for some fresh air. Standing on the service jetty gazing at the tranquil watery scene before them, Peter said, 'It's so peaceful. I can see why Roy chose to come here.'

'So, what now?' asked Tim.

Momentarily lost amongst his surroundings, Peter replied, 'I just need to keep searching for that file. It has got to be somewhere.'

Tim asked if he was driving back to Sparkbrook that evening. He said he wasn't and had booked into a hotel in Melbury. Peggy asked which one.

Peter took a piece of paper from his pocket. 'The White Bear' in North Street.'

'Oh, that's nice, it's a good hotel.'

'I think I might stay for a couple of days. Do a bit of sightseeing and poke around a bit.'

'What do you hope to find?' asked Tim.

Peter shrugged. 'I don't know, but anything's worth a try.'

They walked with him to his car. Peggy said, 'Good luck with it all. If we find anything out, we'll contact you, but it's unlikely.'

Peter smiled. 'Thanks'. Then looking around him said, 'It's so sad to think Roy died in such a lovely place.'

CHAPTER NINE

Black Jack

It was two weeks after Phoebe had spoken to Dwain about George smoking weed, when Black Jack had given Dwain the idea. The double seater touring canoe had been unused for some time. It had been named by Zed and Dwain after the notorious highwayman who, along with his accomplice, One Legged Laura, had once robbed boatmen as they passed through the locks. They had both met a grisly end, being hanged from a tree at Melbury Lock.

Now nearly eighteen and nearing completion of their marine engineering course at college and working at the marina at weekends, little time was left to go paddling on the canals. Dwain though, had remembered George once saying that whilst he had been in a one person kayak, he'd never tried a double canoe. This could be the excuse to get him on his own without Zed.

On Friday and Saturday nights George always stayed with Zed on Turtle Two, much to Phoebe's irritation. Occasionally he would go with the boys to help out at the marina, but more often than not would remain on the boat studying towards his A levels; a stipulation of his mother, Lady Barrington Gore. Dwain's opportunity came unexpectedly.

A friend of Tim's from the marina had bought another narrowboat, which was currently in the dry dock at Boswell's Yard, some miles from Tiddledurn. A recent survey identified thinning of the hull, requiring some over plating. He had asked Tim to complete the task. Already having enough work maintaining the small marina hire fleet, Tim was reluctant to go. Peggy though had intervened, insisting it would do him good to get away for a day. So, he agreed. As he had recently been teaching Zed and Dwain the skills of welding he decided to take them with him.

Space in the Land Rover though became an issue when his friend asked if he could take a few items with him. Much to Tim's irritation these 'few,' plus his own welding equipment had left room for only three people in the front. Dwain had seized the moment and offered to stay behind.

By midday on Saturday the turn round of boats on the small hire fleet was complete. The dutiful team of cleaning ladies had gone home, and the new holiday makers departed the marina. Dwain asked Peggy if he could leave early. It was quiet, so she agreed.

As he left the office she winked. 'Say hello to Phoebe for me.'

He smiled, went outside and phoned George's mobile.

A drowsy voice answered, 'Hello.'

'You weren't asleep, were you?'

'Course not dude, I was revising.'

Dwain laughed. 'Course you were. Right, get your arse moving, we're going canoeing. Meet me at the cottage in an hour.'

'Yeah, right, ok, that's cool.'

Dwain shook his head and rang off. 'Lazy sod.'

George arrived later wearing a tee shirt, jogging bottoms and trainers; his unticy mop of brown hair in need of a comb.

'Where's Zed?' he asked.

'He's gone somewhere with Tim. Come on.'

They went round the back of the cottage where Black Jack sat upturned on a rack. They lifted it off and flipped it over. George puffed. 'Blimey, it's heavier than I thought.' Dwain went into a shed and came out with two paddles and buoyancy aids which he dropped into the canoe.

'Right come on, let's go.'

They carried Black Jack through the garden and down to the water's edge beneath the lock. Whilst George zipped up his buoyancy aid, Dwain knelt down and held the canoe close to the grassy bank. 'Now keep down low and sit on the back seat.'

Taking no chances of a ducking, George gingerly stepped in, holding tight to the gunwales. Dwain passed him a paddle. Then using his to stabilise the balance, moved in front of him. 'Ok, let's go.'

He pushed off with the paddle.

George yelled, 'Bloody hell, it's a bit wobbly.'

Dwain laughed. 'It won't be when we get going. Now follow me with the paddle, or we'll go round in circles, and don't dig too deep.'

Making forward momentum they moved towards the middle of the canal. Tim's two tame swans, Sammy and Sheena eyed them lazily from beside the towpath. A short way along they passed the field where the little donkey always came down to the gate for a carrot, but this time he didn't. Dwain wondered what had happened to him.

It was a warm afternoon, and a gentle zephyr breeze rustled the leaves of the waterside trees. Dwain, his dark skin able to withstand the sun's bright barbs, removed his shirt. George felt a twinge of excitement at the sight of his toned upper body, with small beads of sweat forming between his shoulder blades.

The surrounding silence was broken only by the kiss of the paddles on the surface of the water, and the occasional bleating sheep or lowing cow. George soon got the hang of it, saying, 'Hey man, this is really cool.'

As they exited the narrow bridge hole alongside Muckle Farm, Dwain, pointed out where Rocket Ron and Rose used to moor their boats. George remarked that the derelict buildings looked creepy.

Dwain chuckled. 'It's certainly got history. I'll tell you about it one day.'

There was a short straight where a huge three arched viaduct crossed the canal. 'I wonder how many bricks it took to build that?' pondered Dwain.

The steerer of an oncoming narrowboat waved to them as they passed the place where Peggy's boat, Turtle One, had caught fire one night. A mile before they reached the entrance to Harry Martin's marina, there was a wide bend. On one side a tall red bricked Georgian house with a high hedge, dominated the space. Opposite, a meadow tipped gently down towards the canal. Several horses from the nearby stables drank lazily at the shallow water's edge. Suddenly Dwain back paddled to change the direction of the canoe.

'Where are we going?' asked George.

Dwain pointed. 'Alongside there.'

Startled, George asked, 'What about those horses, they look mean?'

Amused by his friend's nervousness, Dwain laughed. 'Oh, they'll run off. Me and Zed often used to stop here.'

There was a scrunching noise as the hull of the heavy canoe grounded on the silt. As Dwain had predicted the disturbed horses scattered to the upper reaches of the meadow. The two boys stepped out, pulling Black Jack up onto the dry hoof-impregnated grass. Sitting down beside George, Dwain opened a bottle of cola and some biscuits which he had brought. After offering him some he said, 'Now tell me about the weed.'

Surprised by his friend's direct question George stuttered, 'How do you mean dude?'

Little ever changed at Boswell's Yard. Although Tim had been back several times it had been six years since Zed was last here. The heap of old cars had expanded to include a tractor and coach. The rusting crane without doors was still parked on its lorry alongside the water's edge. It was used to lift boats out into the yard. Several of them were languishing neglected on the dusty ground; their hulls having not been brushed by the canal for years.

On the far side piled against a wooden fence, was a stack of discarded oil drums and old engines, their shapes being slowly consumed by coarse wild grass and tangles of creeping weeds. Avoiding the deep ruts in the uneven surface, Tim drove the Land Rover through the gates and parked by the old caravan which Jack Boswell used as an office and home.

Tim's friend, Bernard, owner of the new boat 'Ranika' was keen to see his latest acquisition, so he headed across the yard towards the dry dock; a deep cavernous concrete pit, topped by a corrugated roof.

Tim told him, 'We'll be in the office.'

He banged on the door and went in. As with the untidy yard outside, it was as Tim remembered it previously. Jack Boswell's office by contrast, made Harry Martin's administrative system look efficient. Tim grinned. Peggy would have a fit. The surface of the desk was awash with different coloured folders, stained by oily fingerprints, old magazines and used plastic cups. On the floor were two bowls marked, 'Dogs', though there were none in sight. Beside them a pair of dirty steel toecap working boots: a green metal filing cabinet with an open drawer stood to one side. Eyeing this chaos, Zed said, 'Maybe they've been burgled.'

Tim was just about to respond when, from behind, a gruff voice said, 'Who's been burgled?'

Tim and Zed turned to see the slender figure of Jack Boswell framed in the doorway. His ragged oily, brown overalls, which had fitted once, now hung from him like a shroud and his once chubby features sagged below his prominent cheek bones.

Tim said, 'Blimey Jack, I didn't recognize you.'

'Good to see you Tim. It's been a long time.' He laughed. 'The quack said you either lose weight and cut out the beer and fags or you'll be in a box. So here we are.' He stepped inside and focused his eyes on Zed, remembering him from his mop of ginger hair and freckles.

'This is never your little stowaway?' Zed blushed. Tim smiled at Zed. 'It is, though he's not so small now.' Crossing the room to a round table where there was a kettle and cups Jack asked, 'Anyone for a brew?'
Tim smiled. 'Always. Nice and strong please.'
Zed declined the offer.
Speaking as if Zed wasn't there, Jack said, 'I thought you were sending him back to London.'
Tim laughed, 'We were, but fortunately for us, fate had other plans.'

Leaving the two men to reminisce, Zed said he was going across to the dry dock to see the boat 'Ranika.' The sixty foot trad stern narrowboat, painted royal blue with maroon coach lines, was sitting on heavy wooden sleepers in the drained dock. Zed leaned on the metal safety railings which surrounded the edges of the deep pit. Bernard, the boat owner, was below standing beside the dried hull which had earlier been cleaned by pressure washer. On the floor several square cuts of steel were waiting for Tim to weld them on.
Calling down to him Zed asked, 'Nice boat, are you going to live on it?'

'That's the plan, now that the wife's gone.'
Thinking she had died, Zed said, 'Oh, I'm sorry.'
Bernard laughed. 'No. Not like that. She gave me a choice, either her or the boat. I chose the boat.'
Zed nodded. 'Oh right.'

It was early evening when Tim and Zed eventually left Boswell's Yard to return to Tiddledurn. Bernard had offloaded his belongings from the back of the Land Rover onto the boat. Now that the over plating on the hull was complete, it could be re-floated and start the journey to its mooring at Harry Martin's marina, two days cruising away along the canal.

It had been a long day and both Tim and Zed were tired and dirty. For a time neither spoke, watching from the windows as the countryside unfolded before them. The sun was setting to the west, throwing a warm orange tinge to the sky. The vivid greens of fields and bushes melting into grey as the light gradually faded.

Then Zed asked, 'Why was Peg so spooked about that bloke coming the other day?'

Without diverting his eyes from the road Tim asked, 'What bloke?'

'The one asking questions about Roy Coombs.'

Tim said nothing. Stopping at a set of traffic lights, the awkward void was filled by the stationary chug of the 1.6litre petrol engine. Zed looked across at Tim. One of his large hands rested on the steering wheel, the other thoughtfully tapped the top of the gearstick. Zed thought it best not to ask the question again.

The lights turned to green, and they moved off. Still Tim said nothing. A short way along the road was a wide layby, with several lorries parked up for the night. Tim pulled in behind one, stopped and turned off the ignition. Shifting in his seat to face Zed, he said, 'We were trying to protect you and Dwain from the awful reality of what really happened to Roy Coombs.'

'How do you mean?'

'The explosion wasn't accidental. You remember I went to the inquest in Melbury?'

Zed nodded.

'Well, all the forensic and police evidence points to the theory that some sort of device was planted on his boat, deliberately designed to kill him.'

Wide eyed in disbelief, Zed asked, 'What like a bomb?'

Tim sighed. 'Exactly that, lad.'

Zed stared blankly through the split windscreen of the old Land Rover. Then as if his young mind refused to compute the enormity of what Tim had told him he asked, 'Why do those lorries park with their rear doors open.'

Thrown by the irrelevance of the question Tim took a minute to respond. 'It's to show potential thieves that there's nothing in there worth nicking.'

Almost disinterested in the answer Zed said, 'Oh, right.' Then asked, 'Why did they want to kill him and who was that man?'

Tim started the engine and turned out onto the busy main road. Between there and when they arrived home at the cottage, he explained to Zed the whole story so far about Roy Coombs.

CHAPTER TEN

Threatened

George was uncomfortable being questioned by Dwain.

'Look mate, it's cool if you want to smoke weed, that's your choice. But we both know the stuff's not cheap.'

George shrugged indifferently. 'So what?'

'So, where you getting the dosh from to buy it, and who from? Phoebe said you couldn't afford that from the allowance your parents give you.'

Irritated George asked, 'So, she put you up to this?'

Dwain eyeballed him. 'Nobody put me up to anything. I'm asking you as a mate, before you get yourself into a pile of crap you can't get out of.'

Realising Dwain was deadly serious, George stared down blankly at the dry grass.

'There's this new boy in the sixth form. He's pretty cool and I wanted to hang with him. He was talking about smoking weed at a party, then asked me if I'd tried it. I said I had once.'

'And had you?'

George shook his head. 'No. Anyway, the next day he brought some reefers in. During the lunch break we went over the park and had a smoke. After that he brought more every day for a week. He even gave me a few to take away with me.'

'Was that the tin you had in the field the other night?' asked Dwain.

George nodded. 'I just thought he was being friendly, he's a cool guy.'

Dwain smiled at his friend's gullibility. 'And then when you've got a taste for them, you have to pay, right?'

'Yeah, I told him I couldn't afford to. He said if I helped him out, they wouldn't cost me anything.'

Dwain had a bad feeling where this was going.

George continued. 'He said all I had to do was recruit some users and pass their details to him.'

'And did you?' asked Dwain.

'Yeah, just a few of my mates in the sixth form and some of those blokes down the park.'

Dwain stared in disbelief. 'What blokes, who are they?'

'I don't know. They're always dossing about in there.'

Dwain felt like slapping his friend. 'Are you bloody crazy man? That's dealing! Apart from being expelled from school you could be nicked by the old Bill and end up with a criminal record.'

George stuttered as he tried to defend_himself 'I'm not supplying them, just passing their names on to…..'

Dwain interrupted him. 'Yeah, I've got it, your cool mate.' He stood up. 'You were recruiting people for him George. That's just as bad. You're as guilty as he is.'

Sensing his friend's anger, George deflated like a punctured tyre. 'I know,' he said sullenly. 'I told him I didn't want to do it anymore.' His voice faltered. 'He got really vexed Suddenly he slammed me against the wall with his arm across my throat. I couldn't breathe. He's a lot bigger than me. Then he said I'd be pissing off his suppliers, and unless I wanted them coming after me, I'd better carry on.'

Dwain asked angrily, 'So, he threatened you big time?'

George nodded sullenly. Blinking back tears he said, 'Yeah, I was shaking man. I thought he might have a blade or something.' He paused. 'You won't tell Zed or Phoebe, will you?'

Grabbing George's arm, Dwain yanked him up to his feet, then taking hold of the neck of his tee shirt pulled him roughly towards him.

'No, I won't tell them. But this shit stops now, no more! Got it?'

Half expecting a punch George babbled, 'Yeah Dwain, no more, I promise. But what about........?'

'Leave that prat to me,' said Dwain, letting go of George's tee shirt. Momentarily the two boys stood looking at each other. Then Dwain smiled. 'Shall we finish off the cola and biscuits?'

George relaxed and they both sat back down on the grass, though he was keeping a wary eye on two inquisitive horses that had now crossed the field and were viewing the intruders from only a few feet away. From across the canal, a clattering chain saw pierced the silence and blue, grey bonfire smoke appeared above the roof of the red bricked Georgian house opposite.

Dwain took out his phone and checked the time. 'We'd better be heading back, before it gets dark.' As they slipped on their buoyancy aids, George put his arm around Dwain's shoulder. 'Thanks dude, you're a pal.' Dwain laughed. 'Don't be so soft, but you've got to get a bit more street wise mate.'

As they pushed the canoe from the grass into the shallows Dwain said, 'You jump in the back, and I'll push off.'

Tim and Zed still hadn't returned from Boswell's yard when Dwain and George reached the lock by the cottage. Lifting the canoe from the canal they turned it over to get rid of any water then carried it across the lawn placing it on the rack by Tim's workshop. After stowing the paddles and buoyancy aids in the shed they went into the cottage. In the sitting room Peggy was at the dining table surrounded by a stack of marina invoices and an open lap top. Betty, Zed's gran, her hands covered in flour was as usual in the kitchen preparing dinner. It was a task she relished and often joked, 'I'm not good at much, but I can cook.' Which they all bore testament to.

Peggy looked up from her work as Dwain and George came into the room. 'I thought you were meeting Phoebe this afternoon?'

Dwain chuckled, 'That was your wicked mind Peg. No, me and George went canoeing.'

'Oh, right. Well, it's good to see Black Jack being used again. Did you enjoy it George?'

'Yeah, it was cool.' He smiled at Dwain. 'Though not quite what I was expecting.'

Peggy asked why. Quickly, Dwain said, 'Oh, we stopped at the meadow, and he didn't like the horses.'

She laughed. 'Oh, they won't hurt you. Mind you I have the same fear of cows.'

They flopped down on the sofa. 'What time will Tim and Zed be back?'

Peggy was about to answer him, when they heard the distinctive growl of the Land Rover engine coming along the track. Seconds later the beam of the headlights illuminated the front lawn.

Tim and Zed had hardly stepped through the front door when Peggy shouted, 'Get those muddy boots off.'

'Christ, give us a chance woman,' retorted Tim.

'How did it go?' asked Dwain.

Stripping off his dirty overalls Zed said, 'Yeah, alright. What you two been up to?'

George blurted out, 'We've been canoeing.'

'Oh, I see, while we've been slogging you've been lolling about. No wonder you were eager not to come with us.'

Dwain didn't want to elaborate on the real reason why, so said nothing.

Zed called out, 'Hi Gran.'

She put her head around the door. 'Oh, you remembered I was here then?'

Moving into the kitchen he kissed her on the cheek. 'You'll always be here Gran.'

She laughed. 'I'm not sure about that, love.'

Before sitting down in his favourite chair by the fireplace, Tim tapped Dwain on the head. 'How about a brew for a working man?'

Dwain stood up. 'Sure Tim, nice and strong.'

'Is there any other way lad?'

Betty shouted from the kitchen, 'dinner's nearly ready.'

'Are you staying, George?' asked Peggy.

Having smelt the mouth-watering aromas wafting from the kitchen he answered, 'That would be great Peg, thanks.'

It was gone ten o'clock when Tim drove Betty home to her flat in Tiddledurn. The three boys left the cottage shortly afterwards to walk back to their boats. It was only a short distance, but the moonless, caliginous sky obscured the narrow towpath. Stumbling along the uneven ground, they wished they had taken up the offer of Tim's torch. They flinched as branches, like ghostly fingers reached out and touched their shoulders. George, not as used to the darkness as his two friends, clung tightly to Zed.

The welcoming lights from the windows of Rocket Ron's boat told them they were near to Turtle Two and Rose's old boat. In the darkness, Zed fumbled to find the zip on the cratch cover.

'Come in Dwain I've got something to tell you about Roy Coombs.'

Unlike Rose's old boat, which Tim had internally renovated for Dwain to live in, Turtle Two's interior was unchanged since Peggy had bought it. The floor was covered with panelled wood, topped by a large thick rug. There was a matching dark blue sofa and small chair. A Squirrel solid fuel stove stood in one corner, a television in the other. A small fitted kitchen which included an oven and fridge stood at one end. For teenagers, not normally the tidiest of people, Zed and Dwain kept the boats remarkably clean, which was no doubt due to Betty's weekly inspection. Zed and George sat on the sofa, Dwain in the chair.

Zed began, 'On the way back from Boswell's yard, Tim told me Roy Coombs' death wasn't an accident. The police think the explosion was caused by a bomb.'

Surprised, Dwain asked. 'What, he was murdered?'

Zed shrugged, 'Sounds like it yeah.'

Flippantly George said, 'Wow that's some way to snuff someone out. Boom!'

'It's really weird man that something like that can happen in sleepy Tiddledurn; maybe in London, but not here. Do the police have any Idea who might have done it?' asked Dwain.

Zed shook his head. 'Tim didn't say, but I doubt it.'

'Maybe he was a secret spy and the Russians bumped him off. Like what happened to that bloke in Salisbury,' said George.

Dwain laughed. 'You've been watching too many films dude.' He yawned. 'Oh well, I expect we will know more soon. Right, I'm knackered. I'll see you tomorrow.'

As he stood up to go he winked. 'Behave yourselves you two.'

After he'd left the boat George moved closer to Zed. 'I do love you dude.' He blushed. George kissed him then slowly slid his hand along Zed's thigh and into his trousers. He gasped and tensed. 'It's alright dude.' Zed relaxed, then leant over and turned off the side light.

Dwain envied George and Zed. At least they could spend the night together, unlike him and Phoebe. It just wasn't fair. Once inside his own boat he threw himself onto the sofa. Outside it was starting to rain. He could hear it tapping on the roof. Even though it was late he took out his mobile phone and texted her.

U still awake
ya reading
what
school stuff
boring
ya
miss u sm
miss you too <3
when will see u
asap
love u, gn x
gn :) x

He closed his eyes feeling flushed with heightened sensitivity across his whole body. Undoing his jeans he ran his hands along his inner thighs and crotch feeling for his stiffened penis. Then groaning he shouted, 'Oh fuck.'

CHAPTER ELEVEN

Fear

Although the Imperial Spice Restaurant in Main Street Sparkbrook, didn't open until midday, the owner, Amit Thakur, was always in the kitchen by eight o'clock. Originally from the City of Chandigarh in Northern India, he and his two chefs needed time to meticulously prepare their popular rich curries and sauces.

There were two doors into the kitchen. One led directly into the restaurant seating area, the second opening onto a large square backyard. Because of the heat from the stoves, this door was left open winter and summer. As they prepared the ingredients for the day's menu, the three men chatted to each other in their native Punjabi tongue. From a wall mounted speaker, radio Sangram played Asian music across Birmingham City. The sweet aroma of aromatic spices filled the air. It was just like any other day.

The younger of the two chefs, in his mid-twenties, was Amit's nephew. He carried a bag of waste out into the back yard. A row of different coloured wheelie bins stood at one end. The music from the radio drowned out his initial shriek of surprise and shock. The rubbish bag dropped to the ground as the young chef was slammed hard against the fence. His hands were roughly secured behind him. Turning him round, one of the attackers held a knife to his throat and hissed, 'Keep 'yer mouth shut.'

Petrified, he nodded.

Taking an arm each the two men pushed him towards the kitchen door, he didn't dare struggle. Having their backs to them, neither Amit nor the older chef saw the intruders approach. The voice was loud and aggressive. 'Oi tosswits. Turn that shit music off.'

Startled they turned to face them. Two white men, one well-built the other taller and thinner, stood menacingly either side of Amit's nephew. The one holding the knife had a wide mouth, a flat nose and sported a tattoo of a roaring lion on his thick neck. The other, had bulging eyes which seemed out of proportion to his thin skeletal face. He wore a baseball cap, and a gold cross hung from his left ear.

With narrowed lips, the knifeman spoke. 'Right, tosswits. We want some information.'
Amit's stomach lurched. He was under no illusion what this was about. The two men pushed the young chef into the kitchen and closed the door. The knifeman, his face contorted with a sadistic grin held the blade close to the trembling chef's cheek. 'Good looking boy. Be a shame to spoil it.'

The older chef nervously asked, 'What do you want?'
The one with the baseball cap pointed at Amit. 'We want to know what your mate Peter Baxter is sniffing about after.'

'I don't know what you mean,' said Amit.
The knifeman shook his head. 'Wrong answer mate.' Then without warning he dug the tip of the blade deep into the nephew's cheek. He screamed in pain, as blood trickled down his neck and onto his crisp white jacket.

Amit shouted, 'Stop please, please. What are you doing?'
The knifeman grinned sadistically, 'Tell me about Peter Baxter then.'

'Alright, alright. But please let him go.'
He nodded. 'Ok.' Releasing his grip, he pushed the young chef violently forward. He stumbled and fell face down on the tiled floor. The man in the baseball cap walked over and put his boot on the lad's neck.

Amit leant against one of the cookers for support. 'All I know is that he's gone to a marina in Wiltshire where Roy Coombs moors his boat.

The knifeman nodded. 'Why?'

Amit shrugged. 'He just said he needed to follow something up.'

Suddenly, the man standing next to Amit's nephew delivered a hard kick to his ribs. He groaned and coiled into a ball. Another kick followed, this time to his kidneys. Winded, he opened his mouth, but no sound came out.

His uncle moved to console him, but the knifeman grabbed his arm, pushing him backwards towards the cooker, just missing a vat of boiling oil. Then kneeling beside the writhing lad, he took hold of his ear. Making a slicing motion with the blade, he said, 'Last time, why's he gone there?'

The older chef shouted, 'Please Amit, if you knew anything tell the man.'

Amit closed his eyes in defeat. 'There's a file.'

'What file?'

'Before Hicks and Ali were convicted, Roy Coombs had been investigating their wider criminal activities and was compiling evidence against them which he would eventually present to the police.'

Still holding the young chef's ear, the knifeman asked, 'So where is the file?'

Amit shook his head. 'Please believe me, I don't know. We assumed it must be with Roy Coombs. That's what Peter's gone to find out.'

The knifeman released his grip and stood up. Walking across to Amit he said chillingly, 'If you're messing with us, we'll be back, and it won't be pretty.' He slapped Amit's cheek. 'Tell Baxter we said hello.' Then both men casually strolled out into the sunshine. Amit's nephew was still lying on the floor trying to breathe. His uncle held a wodge of tissue to the bloodied knife wound on his cheek. Carefully, they lifted him up into the sitting position. The older chef said, 'We must get him to hospital. He needs checking over, and that wound treated.' Then he asked angrily, 'Who were those people? What's going on Amit? We should phone the police.'

Amit snapped, 'No! No police. I'll take him to the hospital. You stay here.'

'But why not? Look what they've done to him, poor boy.'

He sighed. 'I know, I know, but we can't do anything yet. I'll tell you why when we get back.'

They lifted the young chef to his feet, walking him out through the yard to Amit's car. He sat slumped in the passenger seat, his left hand holding a fresh wodge of tissue to his face. Amit climbed into the driver's side, leaned across and secured the seat belt around his nephew.

He closed the door and spoke to his old friend through the car window. 'Please just trust me.'

It would take twenty minutes to reach the Queen Elizabeth hospital in the Edgbaston area of Birmingham. As they left the suburb of Sparkbrook, Amit said to his nephew, 'You have to say it was an accident. That you fell down the stairs in the cellar.'

Confused, he asked his uncle why? Sharply Amit said, 'Because, if you say you were attacked, the hospital will inform the police.' He reached out, placing his free hand on his nephew's thick black hair. 'Believe me. If the police get involved at this stage, we will all be in great danger. Do you understand?'

His nephew nodded. Then a few seconds later said, 'There's one problem Uncle.'

'What's that?'

He smiled. 'We don't have a cellar.'

Smokey Joe lingered for a few days more. There was no rush to return to his manufactured happiness, which was a face he presented to the world. He seemed to find a comforting affinity with the dead souls of St Nicholas Church in Abbotsbury. They spoke his kind of language. He would often wander amongst the tombs and gravestones, occasionally stopping to read one of the faded inscriptions. Many of them were of the past century and the narrow plot had subsided as the coffin and its contents had disintegrated into dust. Nobody came anymore to remember the occupants, or bear testament to their earthly existence. They too had no doubt shuffled from this mortal coil.

The past lives of these people buried beneath his feet fascinated him. The many tales they could tell, and the secrets buried with them. Some had accumulated many years on earth, others departed prematurely. There was one grave in particular nestling beneath the sweeping branches of a willow tree. The occupant was one Victor Button, a journeyman carpenter of this Parish. Born July 10th 1865, died January 22nd 1930. Mistakenly believing a 'journeyman' meant a fellow traveller like himself, Smokey concluded this was a man he could converse with. Each morning he would carry a mug of tea to the wooden bench opposite the grassed over grave. There, with only the hollow cooing of wood pigeons for company, Vic and Smokey would discuss matters close to their hearts. Smokey was keen to know about life in those times, often romanticised as God fearing and less complicated. Vic was amazed to hear of the advancement in technology, in particular the World Wide Web and mobile phones.

It was during one of these conversations that the vicar, walking from the Manse to the church, spotted Smokey in the far corner. He went over to him and sat down. Dressed in his black cassock and dog collar with a silver cross hanging from his neck, he oddly reminded Smokey of a chess piece.

'Cathartic, isn't it?'

Smokey nodded.

'I often pass the time of day with them myself. Particularly the ones I knew before they died and have since buried.'

'And you believe they're in a higher place now?'

The vicar sighed. 'I hope so and that they weren't disappointed.'

'That sounds like doubt to me.'

'Doubt is good Joe. It makes you search for the truth and not be blinded by ideology.'

'And you found the truth in your calling?'

Before answering him, the vicar gazed momentarily across the sun drenched graveyard. 'There are times when I look at the evil in the world and wonder. But surly we must believe in something greater than ourselves, if not.......?' He sighed and stood up. 'I'll leave you to your thoughts Joe. God bless.' Smokey was suddenly engulfed in a wave of loneliness which left him breathless. He could cope with living on a desert island, providing there was a boat on the shore, just in case. But now he felt as if that boat had been washed away by a huge wave, leaving his only mode of escape bobbing beyond his reach. He told himself that this sense of detachment had originated with his years in the army. But in his heart, he knew that wasn't true. He had been the only child to parents of Metro Land, dreary suburbia.

How he had hated the regimentation of it all; the rows upon rows of identical housing; each road with the same height trees, all equally spaced; the routines and family rituals. He remembered his secondary school education with its mind numbing curriculum, preparing kids as factory and military fodder. He only ever had two real friends. The others were imaginary, and over the years they all achieved what he had wished for and failed to attain.

When he was a teenager, he overheard his mother telling a neighbour that he was a loner. He had looked it up in the dictionary. *'A person who likes to do things on their own without other people.'* So, there it was. Now he had a badge to wear, and he had worn it ever since. He sat for another half an hour. Momentarily closing his eyes, he let the soothing wave of warmth and quiet wash through him.

'Right Vic. Better be off, see you tomorrow.' He tapped the top of the gravestone and chuckled. 'Don't go anywhere mate.'

CHAPTER TWELVE

Abbotsbury

Smokey Joe weaved his way along the narrow twisting gravel path to the adjoining field where his tent was pitched. Still wearing the black tracksuit he had slept in, he reached under the flysheet and took out a small gas stove and kettle. His rucksack contained everything he needed and nothing he didn't. Opening the flap, he delved inside for some clean clothes. Taking out a pair of knee length khaki shorts, underwear and tee shirt, he laid them out on the ground.

Pouring the hot water into a bowl, he added some cold from a plastic container then stripped. There was something liberating and primal about standing naked in the open air. With only the tent between him and the Manse, he hoped the vicar's wife wasn't watching from the window. Though, as Driftwood used to say, 'You never see a dead budgie fall out of a cage.' He dressed then combed his long hair and beard.

After re-boiling the kettle for some tea, he lay down on the grass. The clock on the church tower struck eleven. 'Well Driftwood, what do you think? Time to head back?' He could hear his old mate's voice. 'Go for it mush, let's go home.'

That afternoon after a stroll into Abbotsbury village, Smokey walked across to the Manse and knocked on the stout wooden door. It was opened by the vicar who was dressed casually in an open necked, short sleeved shirt and a pair of grey slacks. Smokey laughed. 'Blimey I didn't recognise you.'
He grinned. 'This is my off duty attire. Come in, come in.'

The interior of the sprawling house reminded Smokey of 1950's/60's period dramas he had seen on television. The vicar led him along a passage of dark stained wood past the slow muffled ticking of an old grandfather clock. He recognised a copy of John Constable's the 'Hay Wain' amongst the paintings. A creaky heavy door led into a good sized sitting room. On the far side a pair of double glass doors opened out onto a patio littered with potted plants.

There were two sturdy armchairs and a matching sofa. All three showed the signs of many years use. A huge brick fireplace stood empty with logs piled alongside. The wide mantel piece above was adorned by silver-framed family photographs. Along one wall a bookshelf groaned under the weight of its contents some of which had spilled onto the floor below. A baby grand piano stood in one corner, its lid open, with sheet music arranged at eye level. Two huge rugs, their edges frayed, were laid across the polished oak floorboards.

'Take a seat, and I'll put the kettle on.'

Smokey Joe lowered himself into one of the deep comfortable armchairs.

From the kitchen the vicar called, 'Tea or coffee?'

'Coffee, please.'

Looking around the room Smokey noticed there was one item missing, a television. The vicar returned with a tray holding two mugs and a plate of biscuits. He sat down. 'So, what can I do for you Joe?'

'You don't have a television?'

The vicar laughed. 'No, we don't. Have you come to sell me one?'

Smokey chuckled. 'No, I've come to ask if I can stay another couple of days, if that's alright?'

The vicar smiled. 'Of course, dear boy, stay as long as you like.' He liked having him around, particularly if more robbers returned to steal lead from the roof.

Later the vicar produced two cut crystal glasses and a very good bottle of single malt whisky. Though very different characters and background they enjoyed each other's company. Smokey admired his religious conviction and he, the man of the road's lack of conformity to the system. The vicar lowered himself into the other armchair. 'So, Joe, tell me about yourself,' he asked. Being a bit of an anthropologist went with the job. Savouring its peaty taste Smokey took a sip of the Laphroaig. He felt strangely relaxed in the vicar's company, not something he often experienced with people. So, for the next hour he unloaded the weight of his back story from childhood to present day.

The vicar listened to him intently, occasionally stopping him to clarify a point or two. He noticed how Smokey became emotional when talking of his time in different theatres of war. He had killed men and seen too many friends die or become maimed for life. He didn't though reveal to the vicar how he often woke in a sweat after reoccurring nightmares. Nor how he nearly throws himself to the ground when a car backfires or firework explodes. After recounting one particular memory of his old and now deceased friend Driftwood's antics, the vicar laughed. 'This Driftwood sounds like a real character.'

'He was. A one off and a real friend.'

Eventually the vicar asked, 'So, what's the plan now?'

Smokey thought for a moment then shrugged. 'I don't know. I'm getting a bit long in the tooth to keep trudging the countryside.'

'You say that you rented out the house your uncle left you in Coote's Wood?'

'That's right, and I wouldn't want to live there anyway, it's far too big for one person.'

The vicar took a sip of his whisky. 'And what about your caravan near Old Moor Lock?'

Smokey nodded. 'Yeah, I could go back there, but I dread to think what state it's in after two years.'

'But you do have friends there; Tim and Peggy and others.'

Smokey laughed. 'Blimey you have been listening carefully.'

The vicar tapped his head. 'The little grey cells are still working.'

Smokey continued. 'As I told you, it's as much about having a sense of purpose as a place to live. I suppose I've never really had that since leaving the army.'

The vicar agreed. 'It is so important. I'm dreading retirement.'

Smokey Joe stayed to dinner that evening. The vicar's wife, all tweeds and flower arranging, had returned home at five o'clock. She was a dumpy, motherly character with long grey hair, oozing sincerity. It reminded Smokey of his late aunt, old Mr Coote's wife, who he had spent holidays with in Tiddledurn as a child.

The meal of thick pork chops from the local butcher, followed by apple pie and cream, was superb. It was washed down with a bottle of the vicar's homemade blackberry wine, which wasn't half bad, and stronger than Smokey realised. It was gone ten o'clock when he said farewell to his hosts and staggered back to his tent in the adjacent field. Switching on his torch, he threw off his boots, undressed and crawled into his sleeping bag. 'Goodnight, Driftwood, me old mate. See you in the morning.'

Disheartened, Peter Baxter had returned home from Tiddledurn to Sparkbrook empty handed. Maybe the file of evidence which Roy Coombs had, was destroyed in the fire. If so, any attempt by the police to prevent Hicks and Ali being released from prison, or arrested soon afterwards would be lost. Returning to their home turf, they and their associates would be eager to continue their nefarious activities in and around Birmingham.

The following morning, he had arranged to meet with Amit Thakur and Gerry Carter at the café in Main Street. The two men waited in anticipation to hear if he had contacted Roy Coombs. Over mugs of weak, milky tea, their hopes turned to despair as Peter relayed the story of the journalist's demise. Minutes later, their stony expressions hardened even further as a visibly distressed Amit told of the visit by two thugs to his restaurant. 'I am so sorry Peter. Those animals were beating and stabbing my nephew with a knife. I had no choice and had to tell them about the file. They could have killed him.'

Peter put his hand gently on Amit's shoulder. 'I do understand my friend. We would have done the same in that position.'

In despair Gerry said, 'Christ, so now they will be looking for the file as well then?'

Amit agreed. 'No doubt they will. Do you think the file was destroyed in the explosion?'

'It's a possibility,' replied Peter, 'but I still believe Roy would have secreted it away somewhere safe. Just in case.'

'And without knowing where that is, we've come to a dead end,' added Gerry.

Trying to remain positive, Peter concluded, 'For the time being, yes.'

Gerry stared wistfully into the mug of warm liquid. 'I'm thinking of selling up, I've had enough, I can't take the stress of this anymore. I need to consider my family.'

It was hard for the two men to disagree with him. Initially, he had bravely resisted Hick's and Ali's protection demands. Then one night, following a series of verbal threats, a full can of petrol was poured through his letterbox. It wasn't ignited, but the message was clear. Pay up or else.

Though the police investigated, nobody was ever arrested or charged with the offence. The publican however was under no illusion about who was responsible. Following that near miss, and in fear for his family and business, Gerry had complied with their demands. The three men left the café under the usual scowl of the obese café owner. On the pavement outside Peter said, 'We mustn't give up, not yet. There is one person who may help us.'

In unison they both asked, 'Who?'

When he told them, they laughed in his face.

CHAPTER THIRTEEN

An Honest Copper?

Peter Baxter's appointment with Detective Chief Inspector Bill Collins was scheduled for two o'clock in the afternoon. He was apprehensive as he approached the entrance to Sparkbrook Police Station. His perceived trust in the officer was, after all, based on meeting him only once. But there had been a sincerity about the man, an 'old school' coppers belief in upholding the law. But what if he was wrong? Then Amit and Gerry's cynicism would be well founded, and their objective of keeping Hicks and Ali locked up fatally doomed.

Sparkbrook Police Station was an old red brick building, constructed in the early part of the last century. Above the entrance hung a blue lamp, a feature on every 'nick' in the land since 1816. Many cigarette filter tips and dead matches were pressed into the narrow grass verge outside. No doubt discarded by anxious suspects or their weary investigative pursuant. Heavy boot steps over the years had caused a deep indentation in the concrete steps. Peter pressed the wall mounted button and the automatic glass door slid open with a whoosh.

The once sober space, typical of all police stations, with a heavy wooden counter and dark green linoleum floor, now changed to a corporate style reception area. The authoritative Station Sergeant, with his silver crown above three stripes, replaced with a young woman residing behind a plastic screen. She wore a uniform of sorts, with Police Staff on her light blue epaulettes. Baxter approached the screen.

'Good afternoon. I have an appointment at two o'clock with Detective Chief Inspector Collins.'

'Please take a seat and I'll let him know you're here.'

There was a row of orange plastic chairs against one wall. The floor was wood laminate. A tall rubber plant stood on a stand in one corner and a water dispensing machine occupied another. The two round coffee tables held a scattering of leaflets on different types of crime prevention and domestic violence. It struck him this could just as easily be a doctor's or dental surgery.

A door to the right opened and DCI Bill Collins appeared. 'Hello Mr Baxter. Come through, good to see you again.'

His sleeves were rolled up and a plain tie hung from the unbuttoned collar of a white shirt. Peter stood up and they shook hands. On the way to his upstairs office they stopped at a drinks machine.

'Tea or coffee?' he asked.

'Tea please, no sugar.'

A brown muddy liquid trickled into a plastic cup.

The DCI chuckled, 'It's wet and warm.'

The door to his office was open and Peter noticed the surface of the desk was equally as cluttered as on his last visit. The DCI pointed to a chair opposite his. Peter sat down. Leaning back in his imitation leather chair the DCI said, 'I thought we might meet again.'

Peter smiled. 'Thanks for seeing me so promptly. I'd like to discuss further with you the Roy Coombs case.'

DCI Collins stood up, crossed the room, and closed the door. 'Carry on Mr Baxter, I'm listening.'

'I located the marina in Wiltshire where Roy Coombs moored his boat.'

The detective looked surprised. Peter continued. 'Apparently, he died in a boat explosion.' He paused. 'But you knew that didn't you?'

The detective didn't answer the question, instead he said, 'Mr Baxter, for the last thirty years I have rubbed shoulders with most of the scumbags in this city. In most cases, where a crime has been committed, we have been able to bang them up. But, thanks to influential friends and bent lawyers, Hicks, Ali and their associates had been untouchable. That was until their conviction two years ago, and it was only secured due to the compelling evidence of Roy Coombs. Even those on their payroll couldn't argue that one away. Do you understand me?'

Peter Baxter nodded. 'Yes, you're telling me they're well protected.'

He paused. 'Even by some of your own colleagues?'

The DCI sighed. 'I dislike it as much as you. But it's where we are.'

'Do you have any idea how much material Roy Coombs had collated?'

The DCI shook his head. 'Not really, and even if I did it would have been impossible to present it as evidence at their trial. Not without thorough investigation beforehand and establishing its credibility.' He smiled sardonically. 'Remember Mr Baxter, as odious as these people are, they are entitled to a fair trial. Everything in court must be proved beyond reasonable doubt.'

Peter thought for a moment. 'So even if the evidence in the file is overwhelming, you wouldn't be able to arrest them on release from prison?'

The DCI tapped his pen on the glass ashtray, now containing paper clips and drawing pins. This familiar object transported him back to a bygone age, when a comforting cloud of smoke clung to a yellowed ceiling and a bottle of Famous Grouse Whisky nestled in his desk drawer.

For the briefest moment he studied the strained and concerned face of Peter Baxter, trying to imagine the pain he and his friends had been through at the hands of these villains. The question now was just how much should he reveal to him. He sucked the end of his pen, imagining a deep and comforting intake of nicotine into his lungs.

'Mr Baxter. With regards to 'just' the file....'

Surprised at this apparently casual remark Peter interrupted him. 'How do you mean 'just' the file, surely it is central to this?'

The DCI held up his hands. 'Please hear me out sir.' He continued. 'Yes, the collation of evidence by Roy Coombs is important and we take it very seriously. But based on that alone we couldn't hold them for long without a charge, and they would be released on bail under investigation.'

Peter Baxter sighed. 'So, they could be out on the streets for weeks.'

The DCI replied cautiously. 'That is what we are trying to avoid.'

Intrigued Peter asked, 'How do you mean?'

Before answering he pointed to Peter's empty plastic cup. 'Another?'

'Yes please.'

The DCI laughed. 'You're a brave man, I won't be a minute.'

After the DCI had left the room Peter sat pondering on his remarks. Was there more at play here than he knew of? Suddenly he felt a wave of gut wrenching despair. If there was no end to this, would he and Amit Thakur be forced to follow Gerry Carter and sell up their businesses to escape the inevitable.

Hearing a commotion from outside Peter stood up and crossed to the window. It looked down onto the rear yard of the police station. Three officers were struggling to extricate a kicking and screaming handcuffed man from the back of a van. He watched for a few minutes as they forcibly carried him into the building.

A voice behind him said, 'Bloody low life animals, no doubt drugs or drink.' DCI Collins put the drinks on the desk and sat down. 'No biscuits I'm afraid, budget cuts.'

97

'I don't know how you deal with that crap all day.'

The DCI sighed. 'It's a different job now from when I joined. People have no respect for the police anymore.'

Peter sipped tea from the plastic cup. 'There is something else you need to know.'

'Oh, what's that?'

'Hicks and Ali's people know Roy Coombs' file of evidence exists.'

'How's that?'

Peter explained about the recent visit of two thugs to Amit's restaurant.

The DCI replied thoughtfully, 'He did the right thing in the circumstances. These people are capable of anything these days.'

'That's true,' agreed Peter. 'Amit also told them where Roy Coombs moored his narrowboat in Wiltshire.'

The DCI pensively sipped his coffee. 'Mr Baxter. You asked what I meant when I said 'just' the file.'

Peter nodded.

'What I am about to tell you is in the strictest confidence. Do we understand each other?'

Again, Peter nodded. 'Yes.'

'The file, whilst important is only one part of an ongoing investigation into Hicks and Ali. You may not be aware, but the import of crystal meth is the latest scourge to hit this country. We know that Hicks and Ali and their associates are central to the distribution of this in the Midlands area. Therefore, other national agencies than ours are involved in this investigation.' He paused. 'With regards to them discovering the location of Roy Coombs, we already had Intel to suggest they knew that.'

'But, how?'

'That, I'm afraid, is still subject to investigation. So, I can't say anymore.'

'Shouldn't the local police give the people at the marina the heads up, they might get a visit.'

The DCI shook his head. 'Might be difficult. The local boys have no idea we had Roy Coombs there under protection, or why. It could get messy, politically. In the mean time you need to keep a low profile for a few weeks. We don't want you having an unfortunate accident. You said they've already been to your shop. Believe me, they'll be back.'

The thought sent a chill down Peter's spine.

The DCI stood up. 'Right, I'd better get on.' He pointed to the stack of files on his in tray. 'These won't solve themselves.'

They shook hands. 'I'm grateful for your help Chief Inspector.'

'You're welcome my friend. Let's hope it does some good.' He accompanied Peter back along the passage, down the stairs and into the reception area. As Peter exited the front door the DCI called out, 'As the town sheriff would say, "get on your horse and get out of town."'

Peter smiled. It wasn't a bad western imitation.

Stepping out into the afternoon sunshine, he had never thought of the danger to himself before. After all, those things were the stuff of films and television dramas. The black car screeching alongside and masked men forcibly throwing you onto the back seat. Then after being hooded, a speedy drive to a deserted warehouse on the outskirts of town. Here, you would be tortured for information, before a gunman put a bullet in the back of the head. He shuddered at the thought of it.

But this was Sparkbrook in Birmingham, England, not America's New York City and Hicks and Ali were hardly the Mafia's Don Corleone. Even so, as he walked back along Main Street towards his business, he was more vigilant than usual. He stayed well away from the kerb side, eyeing with suspicion every slow moving car, particularly black ones. Likewise, any boarded up shop where he could be abducted and dragged inside.

His betting shop, aptly named, 'Lucky 15' occupied a corner plot on a busy junction. It was, as usual, heaving with punters. The regulars always congregated at the far end, where tall stools stood against a wide shelf holding numerous copies of that day's Racing Post and piles of betting slips. Whilst always happy to take their money Peter felt a twinge of sadness for this group of gamblers whose lives seem to oscillate between his shop and the 'Two Moons' pub further along the road.

He had two members of staff; firstly his assistant, a man in his early sixties, who had been with him for years and who he trusted implicitly, the other, a widowed mother of two, looked after his administration and accounts. Pushing his way through the noisy throng, he entered a code into the security door beside the counter. His assistant winked and smiled broadly. It was a sign that the payouts to punters had been minimal that day. Always music to a bookmaker's ears, so there was something to be pleased about.

CHAPTER FOURTEEN

Little Rich Boy

Dwain left college early that day to walk the short distance across town to his and Zed's old school, Melbury Comprehensive. He had arranged to meet George outside at three thirty. Fortunately, on the opposite side of the road, in front of a row of neat semi houses were several large trees, with girths wide enough to conceal himself behind. George's twin sister, Phoebe, was also in the sixth form at the same school and he didn't want her seeing him. There would be too many questions. Alongside the kerb three single decker school buses were parked waiting to transport those students who lived in outlying villages. A few parent's cars were parked behind them. Dwain took out his phone and texted George his location.

When the final bell of the day rang George was away from the classroom like a greyhound out of the traps. He needed to be able to identify to Dwain the boy selling the drugs. Exiting the gate, he spotted Dwain by the tree and hurried across the road to the opposite pavement. 'Alright dude?'

'Yeah, cool man.'

A few moments later the first wave of young bodies hit the open gates like a tsunami. There were so many of them compressed together it was difficult to identify any one individual amongst the noisy mass; some on bikes, others on scooters poured out onto the pavement. Eagerly smart phones were switched on and messages checked before they dispersed homeward in all directions. But despite scanning the faces there was no sign of the weed boy, as Dwain now called him.

The second group followed behind, still a throng, but more spaced out than before. Dwain and George quickly ducked behind the tree as they saw Phoebe was amongst them, laughing with two other girls as they headed quickly for the bus dropping off at Tiddledurn. Dwain was pleased to see her. At least there weren't any other boys sniffing around.

'Won't she wonder where you are?' he asked George.

'I told her and mum I had cricket practice.'

Having got their correct quota, the waiting buses pulled away towards their destinations. A few students lingered talking by the gate. Further along the teacher's car park started to empty out. The ice cream van which always did good business, closed, and drove off. Dwain asked, 'Are you sure the weed boy was in today?'

'Course dude, I saw him.'

Then Dwain clocked the reason he was hanging back. Two youths had arrived on a motorised scooter. After dismounting, they pushed their helmets onto the back of their heads. Dwain reckoned they were eighteen or nineteen years of age. One took a phone out, tapped in a number, spoke, then returned it to his pocket.

'They're collecting, and guess who from?' said Dwain.

Several late stragglers wandered out. Some wearing games kit, others no doubt having served their time in detention. Two Goth sixth formers sauntered along hand in hand. They wore tight black jeans, black boots, leather jackets and white make up with black mascara. Dwain laughed. 'Bloody weirdos,'

Then George nudged his friend. 'There he is.'

The weed boy was taller than Dwain had imagined. Wearing dark blue tracksuit bottoms, white trainers and a tee shirt, he sauntered cockily towards the gate. An expensive Nordace Eclat black bag was slung across his shoulder. Fist bumping the two waiting scooter lads, he instinctively looked around him. A few words were spoken. Taking off the shoulder bag he delved inside and removed a small brown package. Likewise, one of the lads took an envelope from his pocket and passed it to him. Again, they bumped fists. Then after pulling the helmets back down over their faces, they mounted the scooter and drove off.

'That's blatant dealing man,' said Dwain. 'See the bloody crap you were getting yourself into.'

At first George said nothing then asked, 'What do we do now?'

'We follow him. It's too public to confront him here and I want to see where the little shit lives.'

After following him for twenty minutes, it was clear they were heading for the Roundfield area of Melbury. Like all towns, Melbury had a mixed demographic and had grown considerably over the years. Some, including Tim and Peggy would say too much. Agriculture was its main economic driver, although several light industrial units provided employment for others.

Housing was also equally divided. New estates of private and social homes had been built on surrounding farmland. A rich seam of original 17th century stone properties still existed in the town centre. But Roundfield Park was in a class of its own, with detached property prices starting at two million pounds. Each house was surrounded by considerable lawned gardens with long driveways. Keeping their distance from the weed boy, it took Dwain and George forty five minutes to walk from the school to Roundfield Park. Several times they had to dive into shop doorways or behind walls as he stopped to talk on his phone.

A small wood bordered the entrance to the park where a large sign read 'PRIVATE ROAD. RESIDENTS ONLY.' From here on in Dwain was concerned that he and George would be too exposed. Fortunately, the weed boy turned into the third property in the road; a large, imposing, mock Tudor house. A top of the range Audi CI and BMW sat in the driveway.

'See how the other half lives, dude.'

'Well, I live in a Manor House,' said George.

Dwain laughed. 'Yeah, but it's falling down.'

'Why does he need to sell drugs, with all that bread?' asked George.

Contemptuously Dwain replied, 'He's a little rich boy. Does it for the kicks. Come on I've seen all I need to. He'll wait until tomorrow. Let's go home.'

They walked back through the streets to Melbury market square. After grabbing a burger and milkshake they caught a bus to Tiddledurn village.

Two days later, Dwain again left the Further Education College early. Zed asked him where he was going. Dwain tapped his nose replying, 'business to attend to, don't worry,' though he knew he would. The more he thought about the weed boy scumbag at George's school, the more vexed he became. He and his accomplices preyed on the innocent and didn't give a damn what happened to them afterwards. When living on the estate in South London he had seen how drug addiction had killed Zed's mum and stolen the lives of many others, and he would do what he could to stop it taking hold in Melbury and Tiddledurn,

Having previously followed the weed boy home from school, he knew the route he would take, and where he would ambush him. It was on the outskirts of Melbury where properties thinned to a trickle and the narrow road crossed the canal. The entrance to Melbury Town Football club was adjacent to a small wooded area on one side and a petrol station on the other. A paved path snaked its way through the trees leading to Roundfield Park.

A row of blue wheelie bins stood in front of a small wooden construction, which before the rebuilding used to be the ticket office. Although earmarked for demolition it still stood, albeit precariously. The door had been removed some time ago by local youths no doubt to undertake their nefarious activities. Dwain settled down behind a tree affording him a clear view of the path, turned off his phone and waited for his prey to arrive. It wasn't long.

Chuntering loudly on his mobile phone, Dwain heard the weed boy approaching before he appeared. At least he was on his own which was good. Waiting until he drew level he called out, 'Oi dude, I want a word with you.'

Startled the weed boy turned, but before he could speak Dwain had hold of him in a vice like headlock. Though taller than Dwain he was no match in strength. Despite muffled gasps and futile struggles Dwain dragged him from the path towards the old ticket office. Pushing him through the gap where the door once stood the weed boy fell heavily to the litter strewn dusty floor.

Looking up at Dwain he gasped. 'What the fuck! What do you want?'

He tried to stand. Dwain pushed him back down and slapped him hard across the face. He cried out in pain. 'Is it money, I've got cash in my pocket, here you can have it.'

Dwain hit him again. This time a small trickle of blood came from his nose.

'I don't want your filthy money dude. What I do want is for you to stop selling your shit to kids at the school, and don't try denying it, I've seen you do it.'

The weed boy went pale.

Dwain continued. 'You people make me sick, you've been given everything in life and you still want more. It's just a bloody game to you. Well, I'm telling you creep that if I hear you're at it again I shall go straight to the old bill. I'm sure you parents would be interested to know of your little sideline.'

Now close to tears the weed boy wiped his bloodied nose. 'Alright mate, alright, I promise, no more.'

Leaving the weed boy sprawled on the dirty floor Dwain turned.

'Remember bufflehead, I'll be watching you.'

Outside on the path Dwain picked up the weed boy's mobile phone and threw it into the bushes.

That evening after dinner at the cottage Zed asked, 'So how did you're bit of business go today.'

Dwain grinned. 'Very well.'

CHAPTER FIFTEEN

Time is Running Out

It was eight forty-five in the evening at the Blue Diamond club behind Birmingham New Street station. A few of the early evening regulars were lounging at the tables. The owner, Jimmy Doyle, had his favourite band 'U2' playing over the speakers. It reminded him of his upbringing in Belfast, Northen Ireland, despite the ever present rumble of_incoming and outgoing trains. In Winson Green Prison it was fifteen minutes to lock up. For its inmates, that meant eleven hours shut in a 1.8 by 3 metre cell.

In his office Jimmy held the phone away from his ear as Duncan Hicks raged into it. He and Ali were on the last few weeks of their two year sentence and they wanted nothing to impede their release on licence. Jimmy lit another cigar and waited patiently for the barrage of expletives to subside. He knew better than to interrupt him. Duncan was the more volatile of the two, prone to irrational outbursts and unprovoked violence; his favourite weapon being a brass knuckle duster which he always carried with him and used to great effect, often scarring his victims for life.

Eventually Jimmy said, 'Listen Dunc, we've got it sorted. If this stuff exists, we'll find it. Just chill mate. Keep your head down and you'll soon be out.'

There was a pause then Duncan said quietly, 'I 'ope so mate. We're relying on you.'

Jimmy knew what that veiled threat meant.

A shrill bell rang in the background and a voice said, 'Time to go Duncan.' He grunted reluctantly, 'Laters,' and the phone went dead.

Jimmy replaced the receiver and went through to the bar. U2's music pounded relentlessly off the walls in the dimly lit space. It was filling up, the clientele being mostly Black Country villains and male.

Long legged, skimpily dressed waitresses, all lip gloss and painted nails flitted between the tightly spaced tables, their services often acknowledged by the customers straying hands.

The head barman said, 'Alright boss?'

Jimmy didn't answer. Holding a glass up to the optics, he emptied in a triple vodka, then returned to his office. Lighting another cigar, he put his feet on the desk and studied the piece of paper the two heavies had previously given to him. On it, written in a hand similar to that of a five year old child was the information that they had forcibly obtained from Amit Thakur. Sipping his triple vodka, he pondered this new development about a file and considered his next move. Although time was running out for Hicks and Ali, this had to be handled carefully. It was a time for brains not brawn. Sending in muscle would only attract attention, particularly from the local plod.

Firstly, he needed to find out more about the marina in Tiddledurn. The people who ran it and anybody Roy Coombs may have had contact with when moored there. He switched on his computer to see if they had a website. It did, and not a bad one as sites go. He flicked through the various headings. *'Location, Number of berths available, Services. Boats for sale.'* But it was the section on *'Holiday hire boats'* which caught his attention. He thought for a moment then picked up the phone.

Situated in the suburb of Selly Oak, southwest of Birmingham, was the office of Private Investigator, Mark 'Beaky' Quin, called such because of his long pointed nose. Housed in one small room behind a launderette, its grubby location exemplified the types of cases Beaky became involved in; messy divorces, spying on adulterous partners and of course work for the firm. This always took priority.

When the launderette washing machines were on full spin next door the vibrating dividing wall made conversations almost impossible. The occasional mouse ran untroubled across the floor. A faded, out of date calendar hung on one wall and overhead a single light bulb swung on a brown flex. On the desk an ashtray overflowed with cigarette ends.

Now in his late fifties, his chain smoking and nocturnal lifestyle had left Beaky Quin looking haggard and a lot older than his years. He once had a promising career as a young solicitor, but temptation beckoned, and he got involved in a dodgy property planning scam. Four years later, with his life in tatters, he left prison after being sentenced for perverting the course of justice.

His phone rang. He recognised the number for Jimmy, the owner of the Blue Diamond club so he pressed the green button to answer.

'Hello Beaky, I've got a little job for you.'
Beaky's nose twitched. This meant money, they always paid above the average where a job for the firm was involved.

'How's business? Still got your snout in the trough?' Jimmy enquired.
Beaky smiled. 'Fair to middling, Jimmy. You know how it is these days, scratching a living.'

'So how do you fancy a holiday on a narrowboat in the lovely Wiltshire countryside?'
There was silence then Beaky said, 'Why would I want a holiday on a bleeding narrowboat?'
Jimmy laughed. 'Peace and tranquillity, my son. It'll be good for your health.' That made Beaky's ears prick up, knowing that not to accept would conversely be bad for his health. 'I'm listening Jimmy, go on.'

'I need you to collect some information for me, discretely of course.'

'You know me, discretion is my middle name,' said Beaky.

'And before you ask, you'll get a fair wedge, with a bit more if you score,' Jimmy added.

'Any risks I should know about?'

Again, Jimmy laughed. 'Only falling in the drink. You can swim, can't you?'

'A bit.'

'You'll be fine then. So, you up for it?'

Beaky thought. 'I've got no bloody option. Yeah, ok, when and where?'

'Call into the bar tomorrow and I'll fill you in with the details. You can book it yourself.'

A soft bright light was flooding into the tent when Smokey Joe woke. Normally an early riser he was just about to roll from his sleeping bag when the vicar's voice came from outside.

'Good morning, Joe. Thought you might like a hearty breakfast, and I have something to discuss with you. Come over to the Manse when you're ready.'

Smokey lay for a few minutes watching a spider scuttle along the ridge pole then suddenly it dropped down onto his sleeping bag. Tenderly he scooped it up. Holding it in the palm of his hand, he unzipped the tent flap then crawled out onto the dewy wet grass. 'There you go little fella,' he said, placing the spider on the ground.

A low clinging mist hung over the fields, giving the ruins of the Benedictine Abbey a ghostly appearance. Smokey stood for a moment drinking in the tranquillity. Suddenly, piercing the otherwise silent landscape the clock on the church tower struck nine. He stretched then gasped as a muscular pain assaulted his lower back. In need of a mug of tea and a wash he lit the small camping stove, putting a pot on top to boil some water.

Dressed in an old grey tracksuit he sauntered slowly across the field towards the Manse. A chorus of birdsong came from the tall, surrounding trees. The heavy wooden front door was partly open. He pushed it and called out, 'Hello.'

The welcoming aroma of sizzling bacon came from inside. In the kitchen two places were laid on a large round table. The vicar hovered in front of a dark green Aga, a tea towel thrown over his shoulder.

'Sit down dear boy, sit down. It's nearly ready, help yourself to tea.'

A large white teapot stood next to two mugs.

'I thought your wife would be here', asked Smokey.

The vicar laughed.' Good grief no, she left early. It's the Woman's Institute ramble today.'

Smokey said nothing, thinking. 'I bet that's a barrel of laughs.'

After finishing breakfast and his third mug of tea, Smokey patted his full belly. 'Well, that was some fry up, thanks.'

'I'm glad you enjoyed it Joe,' said the vicar. 'Now, down to business. All the land around here is owned by the Ilchester estate, 15,000 acres in all, which includes the swannery and subtropical gardens. A large part of their income comes from organising pheasant shoots for rich people. As you can imagine, protecting all this, particularly against poachers, is a huge undertaking. Last year, they had to cancel shoots because some animal rights people broke in and released all the chicks.'

Smokey grinned. 'Good food for foxes.'

The vicar drank some tea. 'Exactly.' He paused to acknowledge the confusion on Smokey's face.' You're wondering why I'm telling you this?'

Smokey nodded. 'I am, yes.'

'Well, the estate manager is a regular worshiper at the church, and I happen to know they are looking for a full time assistant gamekeeper.'

For a moment Smokey just stared at the churchman then laughed out loud. 'What, you think..........?'

The vicar interrupted. 'Yes. You Joe. It would be perfect. Give you a sense of purpose. There's also a rent free cottage on the estate and given your past experiences......! Poacher turned gamekeeper.....' the vicar chuckled. Smokey felt slightly embarrassed, forgetting that under the influence of a good malt whisky he had told him that.

The churchman stood up to refresh the teapot. 'I'm not asking you to decide now Joe. Just promise me you will think about it. I am sure if I recommend you, there won't be a problem.'

CHAPTER SIXTEEN

The Mole

Peggy rarely took an instant dislike to anybody, but the gaunt little man in the grubby coat who came to the office that Saturday morning was an exception to the rule. She couldn't put her finger on it but there was something uneasy about him. Beaky Quin dropped his bag onto the floor. 'Morning, I booked a narrowboat for the week, Colvin's the name,' he said with monotone intonation. She recognised a Birmingham accent, not her favourite dialect.

Peggy forced a smile. She went to the desk top computer, selected the bookings section and scrolled through. 'Ah yes Mr Colvin, you booked online last week.'
He grinned. 'It was a last minute decision, get away from the big city.'

She handed him a form and a pen. 'If you could complete that for me and pay the balance less your deposit.' As well as an assumed name he also falsified his Birmingham address. She was surprised when he handed it over in cash. He chuckled. 'I should count it love, never be too sure.'
Peggy bristled at being called love. 'So, have you done much boating before?' she asked.

He laughed. 'No, apart from a pedal boat in Canon Hill Park, that's it.' Taken aback, Peggy asked, 'So, you have no experience of handling a narrowboat or operating the locks.' He shook his head. 'None love, but don't worry I'm not going anywhere.'
Confused, Peggy said, 'Sorry I don't understand.'

'Well, if it's alright with you I just want to stay in the marina. Use it as a sort of base whilst I do a bit of sightseeing.'

Peggy shrugged. 'Well, it's certainly unusual, but yes that will be ok.' She paused. 'Wouldn't it have been cheaper staying in a bed and breakfast?'

'I just fancied something different,' he said scratching his long nose.

Peggy nodded. 'Oh, right, I'll get someone to take you over to the boat.'

She left the office and went round the side where Tim had his Portacabin workshop. After she had gone, Beaky quickly scanned the office layout looking particularly for the location of filing cabinets and evidence of a burglar alarm. Loud music from Kiss FM blared from the interior of the workshop. Clearly Tim wasn't there otherwise, and despite the boy's protestations, Classic FM would have been on the radio. On the work bench a long steel rod was clamped in a vice. As Zed held the wavering end Dwain worked through it with a hacksaw.

Peggy shouted, 'Are you two deaf?'

Seeing her standing there, Zed reached up to the shelf and turned off the radio.

'There's a man in the office who has booked 'Moorhen' for a week, could one of you take him over and show him round.'

Zed said, 'I'll go Peg.'

He followed her back to the office. 'This is Mr Colvin,' Peggy said.

Quin grinned. 'Alright son?'

Peggy took a key from a wall board and handed it to Zed.

'Follow me,' said Zed.

The hire boat moorings were on the far side of the marina. At the end of the central pontoon was a blackened scar on the wooden slats. Quin asked. 'What happened there?' Although of course he knew.

Having been told by Tim not to discuss the tragedy with anyone, Zed just shrugged, 'Oh, just a small fire.'

Quin shrugged back. 'You can never be too careful, nasty thing fire.'

The two berth narrowboat 'Moorhen' was the third of the hire boats moored alongside the pontoon. Quin, alias Colvin, stopped, took a cigarette from a packet and lit it.

'You smoke?' he asked holding out the packet to Zed. He declined.

He stood for a moment looking across the marina. 'Pretty nice 'ere, peaceful like.'

Zed agreed. 'Yeah. It's cool.' Zed used the key to unlock the bow end door.

'Come through Mr Colvin,' he said beckoning inside.

Quin looked around the compact cabin. 'Very nice.'

Zed asked, 'Peggy tells me, you're not going out on the canal?'

'Yeah, that's right,' he laughed. 'Haven't got me sea legs.'

'Ok, I won't bother going through the engine checks then.'

'Just as well, I'm no good with engines.'

Zed continued. 'Well, it's pretty straightforward then.' He showed him the gas cooker and central heating, not that he should need it. 'You're connected to 240v shoreline, so you don't need to worry about draining the batteries.' He pointed to a small closet. 'That's the heads.'

Baffled, Quin asked, 'The what?'

Zed laughed. 'Oh sorry, it's a nautical term, means the loo.' Pointing towards the stern he said, 'The bedroom is in there.'

Quin, alias Colvin, gave him a thumbs up. 'Great stuff son, I'll get settled in then.'

As Zed was about to leave the boat Quin asked, 'I've got a lot of cash with me, and I don't want to carry it about. Do they have a safe in the office?'

Zed nodded. 'Yeah, Mr Colvin. You'll have to see Peggy or Tim.'

He smiled. 'Will do mate.'

Back at the office Zed said, 'He's weird, that bloke.'

Peggy laughed. 'I'm glad it's not just me who thinks that.'

It had been two days since the vicar's suggestion of a job as an assistant gamekeeper on the Illchester estate, and Smokey Joe needed to decide soon. A warm breeze drifted across the field as he lay on the grass contemplating his past and future years. His bedding role consisting of a sleeping bag and carry mat were thrown over the ridge pole of the tent airing. A plate and frying pan lay in a washing up bowl following his earlier bacon sandwich breakfast

A pile of freshly cleaned clothes lay nearby in a carrier bag, courtesy of the vicar's wife. He had resisted her offer at first saying, 'they might pong a bit.' She had laughed at that. 'Don't worry, our boys were teenagers once, they can't be worse than that.' She recalled them once coming back from the Glastonbury music festival. 'It took me ages just to get the mud out.'

That surprised Smokey as he hadn't visualised them as having children. During his time in the army, he had made many difficult decisions, many of them life changing. But this decision would be different. It would be like shedding an old and familiar skin and stepping into the unknown.

His mind needed no prompting to drift back to fighting the Taliban in Helmand Province, having been deployed there in 2009 as a seasoned sergeant. There was one incident which constantly haunted him, and the cause of his many nightmares. During one patrol he witnessed a native interpreter, with whom he had a real friendship, step on an improvised explosive device. He knelt beside him holding his hand as he died, his legs blown off by the blast. During that awful day he also lost another member of his platoon to a Taliban sniper, he was twenty, just a boy.

The strong scent of the gardenia bush wafting from the vicar's garden reminded him of his holidays as a boy spent at Coote's Wood. Staying with his uncle and aunt were some of the happiest days of his life. He still bitterly regretted losing contact with them for so long, but it was too late now they had both passed away.

He fondly remembered meeting Tim for the first time. He was older and having been brought up alongside the canals in Tiddledurn, had taught the young townie boy the ways of the countryside, particularly fishing and catching rabbits. This had proved useful during his years of living off the countryside. Since then, he and Peggy had become lifelong friends and supported him a lot after his old mate Driftwood had died.

He opened his eyes, staring up to a blue cloudless sky. 'Well Driftwood me old mate, what do you reckon? Is it time to hang up my boots?'

Although only in his late forties life on the road could be tough, and whilst he could still deal with the physical aspect he was experiencing moments of unnerving despondency and loneliness, particularly after Driftwood's passing.

A grey squirrel scampered across the grass and stopped close to the tent. Smokey laughed. 'Ah, there you are Driftwood.'

The clock on the church tower struck twelve. He stood up, stretched, then winced as his lower back complained. Putting on his wide brimmed hat with the pheasant feather, he looked at the little grey squirrel, now sitting up on its haunches. 'Come on then Driftwood, there is someone I'd like you to meet.' The rodent didn't follow, though Smokey Joe knew his mate was with him in

117

spirit. Crossing the field, he took the short track towards the St Nicholas church and graveyard.

He followed the winding gravel path until he reached the wooden bench underneath the sprawling willow tree. Sitting down he said, 'Here we are Driftwood, meet Victor Button.' He pointed to the grave. A large crow swooped from a nearby tree and landed on the headstone.

He laughed. 'Ah, there you are me old mate, make up your mind.' He sat for some time explaining his dilemma to Driftwood and Victor Button. Eventually, he said, 'Well, there you have it, what to do?'

The crow cocked its head, cawed then took flight, returning minutes later with a discarded shotgun cartridge which it dropped at Smokey's feet. He chuckled. 'Thanks Driftwood I'll take that as a sign.'

CHAPTER SEVENTEEN

Paper Money

Beaky Quin, alias Colvin, sat on the bow end of the narrowboat, Moorhen, gazing across the still silent waters of the marina. Coughing loudly, he spat phlegm into the water then lit another cigarette, his fourth of the morning. Mindful of Jimmy Doyle's warning of discretion, he considered the task before him. Unless he could acquire the office keys, which was unlikely, then the only way was to force entry. Then, there was the safe to consider, he had certain skills, but safe cracking was not amongst them.

There was though, someone he had met whilst in Wandsworth prison who would fit that role perfectly. He took out his phone, scrolled through his contacts then called his ex con friend. After finishing the call Beaky Quin stepped from the narrowboat onto the wooden jetty, then walked along to where scorch marks from the explosion still scarred the wood.

'So, Mr Coombs where did you leave that file?' he voiced his thoughts out loud.

Across the far side of the marina, Quin could see Zed and Dwain making one of the hire boats ready to take over to the service pontoon. He waved to them, but it was not reciprocated. He shrugged. 'Suit yourself.'

It was still early in the day, Tim was outside the office drinking a mug of strong hot tea; Peggy had yet to arrive. As soon as Beaky Quin saw Tim he made a bee line for him.

'Morning, I'm staying on one of the hire boats.'

Tim looked up. 'So, I hear Mr Colvin, but you're not going out on the canal?'

Beaky Quin giggled, repeating the same mantra as before. 'Haven't got my sea legs yet.'

Tim was in no mood for inane prattle and replied tersely, 'It's a bloody canal.'

Slighted, Beaky retreated within his skinny frame then asked, 'I mentioned to your lad about leaving some cash in your safe.'

Taking a gulp of tea, Tim replied, 'No problem.'

Again Beaky giggled. 'I hope it's a strong one?'

Tiring of his fatuous remarks, Tim replied sarcastically, 'Are you talking about the tea or the safe?'

Beaky tittered, 'The safe of course.'

'There's no point in having one if it's not,' Tim replied indifferently. 'Bring the money over to the office when Peggy is here.'

Beaky Quin turned to look as the hire boat 'Kingfisher' bumped along the service pontoon. Tim stood and called out, 'Well done lads.'

Zed and Dwain made the lines secure then turned off the engine.

Watching Beaky Quin walk off in the direction of the car park Zed said, 'He gives me the creeps that bloke.'

This was a sad day for Zed, as 'Kingfisher' along with three other hire boats were all being sold. For many years now they had been faultless workhorses but were now showing their age and becoming expensive to maintain.

Tim put his hand on Zed's shoulder. 'Lots of memories on this boat lad.'

Zed nodded. 'Certainly are, Tim.'

Dwain of course knew Zed's back story and shared his sadness.

Zed, then just eleven, and living with his uncle in a travelling circus had run away. Seeing 'Kingfisher' moored outside a canal side shop, he had stowed aboard. Peggy, who was taking the boat to Boswell's yard for blacking, had found him hiding in the wardrobe. The rest, as they say, is history.

The taxi from Tiddledurn came along the driveway and stopped in front of the office. Peggy stepped out and walked towards them.

'Reminiscing, are we?'

'We should have sent the scrawny little oik packing,' laughed Tim then grabbing Zed in a headlock he said, 'But we love him now.'

Peggy and Dwain were surprised by this unexpected outward show of affection. Peggy asked, 'And where would you be without them today?'

Tim grinned. 'Financially a lot better off.'

Peggy raised her eyes. 'Yes and the graveyards are full of wealthy people.'

Changing the subject Tim continued, 'Right lads, you'd better get her cleaned off, the new owners will be here at midday.'

As he and Peggy walked back to the office he said, 'That Colvin bloke has been looking for you. Says he wants to put some money in the safe.'

After returning from Tiddledurn village Beaky Quin went straight to the boat. He took an envelope from his pocket, filled it with strips of torn newspaper then sealed the flap. Later that afternoon he returned to the office with the envelope.

Peggy looked up from her laptop. 'Can I help you Mr Colvin?'

'I've got the money....' He paused. 'To go in the safe.'

Peggy stood up, holding out her hand she said, 'I'll put it in for you.'

He hesitated in handing it over. 'I'd rather see it secured myself. It's all the money I've got in the world.'

Exasperated, Peggy beckoned him to where the waist high safe stood next to a filing cabinet. As she bent down to open it, he noted the make of the safe, though was unable to see the numbers which she selected on the dial.

Once opened, he handed her the envelope. 'Thanks love, that's a weight of my mind.'

Curtly she asked, 'Is that all?'

He grinned. 'Yeah, ta love.'

Peggy closed the safe door and twisted the dial. 'I'll give him bloody love.' She mouthed to herself.

It had been two weeks since DCI Bill Collins had spoken to Peter Baxter. Now he pondered on the distasteful thought that in addition to the National Crime Agency's main suspect, a very senior detective, there was a possibility that more officers at Sparkbrook Police Station could be feeding information to the associates of Duncan Hicks and Sahil Ali. This clearly may have led to the gang discovering Roy Coombs at a marina in Wiltshire.

There were of course other possible suspects in the force. Certain officers in the drug squad were known to have taken favours from Hicks and Ali over the years, though despite allegations nothing had ever been proved. But they were not involved in, nor had access to the details of 'Operation Ghost' the name given to the highly secret investigation undertaken jointly by the Serious Crime Squad and the NCA. Following the trial and conviction of Hicks and Ali, the protection order for the journalist Roy Coombs had been approved at the highest level and his location known only to members of the Serious Crime Squad, the NCA, and DSU Turner.

Standing up from his desk DCI Collins walked across the room to the window which overlooked the back yard. Looking down on the row of parked police vehicles, he sadly concluded that the informant could possibly be one of his own officers. It did though seem implausible as there were only six of them in his squad. Three of whom, including his sergeant, he had worked closely alongside for many years and would trust them with his life, and on some occasions, he had needed to. The sergeant was also the only one in his squad involved in the covert Operation Ghost.

Collins watched as down below yet another van arrived, transporting more of Sparkbrook's low life to a night in the cells. He sighed. Roll on the next few weeks and his retirement. His wife already had her eyes on a cruise ship holiday, that was after he had re-decorated the house and landscaped the garden. He laughed to himself. 'Might be easier, not retiring.'

Leaving his office, he went out into the corridor and walked along to the coffee machine. He selected a strong black with sugar and waited. Nothing happened. 'For Christ's sake,' he shouted then looked around him before delivering a sharp kick to the bottom of the machine. Instantaneously the black liquid started to pour into the cup. He smiled. 'Bit of brute force always works.'

This was a mantra his old governor in the eighties had installed in him. Sadly, times had changed, now everything is filmed and recorded, often with the rights of the criminal, over-riding those of the victim. He returned to his office, opened his computer and selected the personal files of members of his team. He studied their careers to date, particularly before joining the Serious Crime Squad. He looked at their domestic circumstances, what was their marital status? Was there anything in their lives that might necessitate taking a bribe?

It was getting dark outside. He had been at the station for twelve hours. Taking his jacket from the back of the chair, he turned off his desk lamp and computer then closed the office door behind him. As he walked along the corridor he still found in inconceivable that one of his own could be responsible, after all he had appointed them.

Stepping out of the front door he drew in a deep breath of fresh air, as if relieving himself of the murky taste of criminality. He was about to walk to his car when a voice behind him called. He turned.

Superintendent Warren Turner was standing there like a tailor's dummy in a pristine three piece suit with brief case in hand.

'Glad I caught you, Bill.'

The DCI inwardly groaned. 'Oh yes, why's that boss?'

'Just wondered if you've heard anymore from that Peter Baxter chap?'

Collins shrugged. 'Not a word.'

Turner smiled. 'Just as well, let sleeping dogs lie.'

Bill Collins nodded. 'Absolutely, as you say. Right, must be going.'

CHAPTER EIGHTEEN

The Break In

It was the evening. Beaky Quin had earlier collected his safe cracking mate from Melbury Station, now both men waited patiently in the boat until they saw Tim, Peggy and the boys lock up and the Land Rover leave the marina. Although the break in would be obvious when discovered, Beaky's plan was to return to the boat afterwards. Being seen about in the marina the following day would, he calculated remove any suspicion of his involvement. As they waited for darkness to engulf them, they drank from cans of beer, chain smoked and reminisced on their days in prison. The greasy remnants of an earlier fish and chip supper lay littering the table.

'This should be a piece of cake, there's no alarm on the building,' said Beaky.

His mate asked, 'So, what exactly are we looking for?'

Beaky sniffed. 'Don't worry about that. Just get the bloody safe open and I'll do the rest.'

He pulled open the curtain. Outside the window there was a quarter moon and in the inky silence only the silhouettes of the bobbing moored boats were visible. Beaky finished his can of beer and stood up. 'Time to go, mate. Let's do it.'

Before leaving the boat both men slipped on pairs of Nitrile gloves, popular with professional burglars as they greatly eliminated the risk of leaving fingerprints. Moving carefully along the central pontoon towards the office, his mate jumped as a startled lone heron took flight. On the service jetty a row of ground level lights illuminated the edging and fuel pump. Other than that a welcome blackness surrounded them.

Walking towards the office, Beaky cast a cursory glance around him, just in case. Then, taking a long screwdriver from his pocket he pushed it hard between the frame and the door. The wood was old and soon surrendered to the forceful intervention, emitting a loud splintering sound as the two separated, rendering the lock useless. Beaky smiled. 'We're in mate, easy peasy.'

Both men moved quickly inside the room. Beaky closed the door behind him and pulled down the window blind. Switching on his torch he directed a beam of light around the office. He whispered, 'The safe's over there against the wall, don't take too long.' Slighted, his mate replied, 'You're talking to an expert here.'

Beaky chuckled. 'Yeah, that's why you spent time at Her Majesty's pleasure.'

His mate put on a head torch and got to work on opening the safe. Beaky started sifting through the filing cabinet and desk drawers. Anything slightly unrelated was discarded on the floor. Even now he was unaware whether he was searching for a paper file or a memory stick.

In the cottage at Tiddledurn it was seven o'clock. They had just finished dinner, one of Betty's popular homemade steak and kidney puddings, followed by jelly and ice cream. Tim was sitting in his favourite chair by the fireplace, although being summer no comforting orange flames danced around the logs. Zed and Dwain were in the kitchen washing up, albeit reluctantly. Peggy and Betty relaxed on the sofa, awaiting the next depressing episode of their favourite soap.

Peggy asked Tim, 'What time is your meeting tomorrow?'

He yawned. 'Too early, bloody nonsense bureaucracy.'

For some time now he had complained that the Portacabin workshop at the marina was too small, particularly with Zed and Dwain working there as well. So, after consulting a local surveyor, he had drawn up plans to do away with it and build a new and larger workshop in its place. Firstly, though, he had to obtain planning permission from the local council at Melbury.

Peggy asked, 'Are you sure you've filled in all the application forms correctly?'

Tim barked back, 'Of course, I'm not a bloody idiot.'

Peggy nodded patiently and waited. 'Ok love, if you're sure.'

Tim reflected on her suggestion for a moment then stood up. 'Well maybe you could just cast a final eye over them, just in case. I'll fetch them from the Land Rover.'

Peggy and Betty smiled at each other. As he was leaving the room Zed appeared in the kitchen doorway.

'Can we see the plan's too Tim?'

He turned. 'On one condition lad.'

Zed laughed. 'I know, a strong brew.'

'You know that man too well Peggy,' said Betty.

Minutes later he returned flustered. 'I don't bloody believe it. I must have left them on the desk in the office.'

Peggy said, 'Don't worry love you can get them in the morning.'

He shook his head. 'No, I'll go now. I don't want to get held up in the morning and be late. You know what these jobsworth council officials are like. They'll probably make me wait another six weeks before they see me again.'

Zed came into the room with his tea, but Tim had already grabbed his keys and left. Peggy sighed. 'His memory is getting worse.'

Betty laughed. 'He's not the only one, although I can blame it on age.'

It was Beaky Quin who first noticed the beam of the headlights coming into the marina. He quickly turned off his torch telling his mate to do the same. Kneeling in front of the safe he asked, 'What's up?'

Beaky whispered, 'There's a car coming up the drive. It may just be one of the boaters coming home.'

They waited silently as the vehicle pulled into the car park and stopped. Beaky carefully pulled back the blind. It was difficult to make out the driver in the dark, but as the figure drew closer, he could see the silhouette of a tall well-built man.

He swore, 'Christ, it's the bloke who runs the marina and he's coming in here.'

Panicking, his mate asked, 'What the hell do we do now? I've just got the safe open.'

Trying to stay calm and keep his voice to a whisper Beaky answered, 'You stay kneeling down there where you are, he won't see you in the dark.' Beaky crossed to the desk and picked up a heavy glass ashtray, then positioned himself in hiding behind the door.

Tim took the office key from his pocket. Feeling for the keyhole he pushed it in. That gentle pressure was enough for the damaged door to swing freely open. He cursed at not bringing a torch, though it was obvious that they had had intruders. He stood for a moment listening for any sounds inside. There were none, so he concluded that the burglars, whoever they were, were probably long gone.

This situation was well outside Beaky's league. His hand was shaking, with beads of sweat running down his forehead. Given Tim's size against his, he would only have one chance to disable him. Tim edged the door fully open, then cautiously stepped inside. As he felt for the light switch Beaky swung the ashtray with as much force as he could muster. The blow to the back of his head did not knock Tim out, but as he staggered forward, he fell and hit his head on the corner of the desk rendering himself senseless.

Now scared, Beaky shouted, 'We've got to get out of here fast.'

Standing up his mate asked, 'What about the stuff we came for?'

Beaky, not the most fearless of men, was already outside the door, 'Stuff it. Come on hurry, before he comes to.'

Leaving Tim flat on the floor, the two men ran to Beaky Quin's car and were soon speeding off through the lanes. It was over an hour later, when they just started to relax. A directional sign for the motorway indicated the M4 was close, when Beaky suddenly shrieked.

'Bloody hell, I've left my bag on the boat.'

'Well, we can't go back now,' said his mate.

Incensed at his own stupidity Beaky punched the steering wheel.

'Was there anything with your real ID in it?'

Beaky felt in his pocket for his wallet. 'I don't think so, just a change of clothes.'

At the cottage it was now ten thirty and Peggy was getting worried. She had called Tim's mobile and the office number twice without any response. Zed and Dwain were still there, as was Betty, who Tim normally took back to her flat in Tiddledurn.

Zed said. 'Maybe he's talking to someone in the marina?'

Peggy shook her head dismissively. 'Not this time of night love, and why's he not answering his phone?'

'Why not give it to eleven then phone a cab to go to the marina,' suggested Betty.

Peggy though was not for waiting. 'I know something's wrong. I'll call a cab now.'

It didn't take long for the large saloon car to pull up outside the cottage. Peggy knew the female driver, but then she and Tim were acquainted with everybody in Tiddledurn. Betty said she would wait by the phone just in case. Having explained to the driver the reason for the call, she floored it through the lanes a lot quicker than usual. It took no more than twenty minutes before they were pulling up in the marina car park.

Zed said, 'Look, there's the land Rover.'

He jumped from the cab and ran over to it, then called back. 'He's not in there.' As Peggy and Dwain were getting out of the cab the driver handed her a torch. As she reached the office Peggy immediately saw the damage to the frame and the half opened door.

Dwain nudged her to one side. 'Let me go first Peg.'

Feeling along the wall for the light switch he turned it on. Peggy shrieked. Tim was lying face down on the floor, a trickle of blood oozing from his head.

Sending Zed to fetch a wet tea towel from the kitchen she knelt beside him. 'Tim, Tim, can you hear me?'

After murmuring something inaudible Dwain and Peggy moved him gently into a seated position against the desk. Zed pressed the wet tea towel to his forehead.

Dwain said, 'I'll ring the police.'

'And an ambulance,' added Peggy.

Now starting to regain his senses Tim muttered. 'I don't need a bloody ambulance.'

Peggy was in no mood for an argument. 'Well you're having one, you may have concussion.'

He groaned, more in compliance than pain.

Looking at the mess on the floor and the open safe, Dwain asked, 'What the hell were they looking for?'

Still kneeling by Tim's side Peggy replied, 'Well if it was money, they were out of luck.' Then remembering the envelope which Beaky Quin had given her for safe keeping she asked Dwain to check inside the safe. After carefully rummaging amongst the secured documents, he confirmed it was still there.

She breathed a sigh of relief. 'Thank goodness for that. Tim must have disturbed them before they had a chance to take anything.'

CHAPTER NINETEEN

Vanished

The two uniformed police officers from Melbury town, whilst sympathetic to Tim's plight, were professionally clinical in their observations of the crime scene, of which they had no doubt seen many. They asked the standard questions of the victims when dealing with any break in.

'Have you touched anything?'

'Do you have any idea who might be responsible?'

'What time did you discover it?'

'Is there CCTV?'

But it was the question regarding anything obvious missing which prompted Peggy to mention the money Mr Colvin had given her to look after.

The officer asked, 'Was it taken?'

'Well, that's the odd thing. It's still there, in the safe.'

Putting on a pair of latex gloves he went to look inside.

'Is this it?' he asked, holding up the brown envelope.

Peggy confirmed it was.

'Do you know how much cash it contains?'

Peggy replied that she didn't. 'Though he did say it was all the money he had.'

Placing it on the desk, the officer said, 'Well let's find out shall we?'

He opened the flap and tipped the contents out onto the wooden surface. Astonished, they all stared as shreds of ripped newspaper tumbled out.

The officer smiled. 'I think you've been had. What did you say this bloke's name was?'

'Mr Colvin. He was staying in the marina for a week on one of our hire boats.'

'I can show you where it is,' volunteered Zed.

Both officers followed him outside, making their way along the pontoon to where the narrowboat 'Moorhen', was moored. Minutes later, a second pulsating blue light reflected through the office window as the ambulance pulled up outside. Tim, by now far more lucid than when first discovered lying on the floor, was still protesting at the unnecessary fuss being made.

But oh, how a stubborn heart can be wooed by the sight and care of a young female paramedic!

Kneeling beside him she said, 'Hello sir, my name is Julie. I hear you've had a nasty bump to the head, can I have a look?'

Tim's antipathy to medical intervention faded like a morning mist. After taking some items from her bag, she gently cleaned and dressed the wound.

Relishing the attention, he murmured softly, 'You've got soothing hands miss.'

At the same time her partner was asking him questions to establish his alertness.

'Does he need to go to hospital?' asked Peggy.

The male paramedic replied, 'I still need to check his balance and coordination for concussion, but I think he's going to be ok.' Looking down at Tim he said, 'Let's get you up,' then carefully they both helped him to his feet. Tim could stand unaided, so the paramedic asked him to take a few steps.

'How do you feel?' asked Dwain.

'Not too bad, I'm made of strong stuff son.'

Peggy sighed. 'You've certainly got a thick head.'

Both paramedics laughed.

'They're like this all the time,' said Dwain.

Zed and the two police officers stepped into the bow of the hire boat, 'Moorhen'. Once Zed had unlocked the door he was told to stay outside, then each officer put on latex gloves and went in. One called out. 'Where's the light switch?'

Zed told them it was a roof light above where they were standing. They switched it on. The interior was as Beaky Quin and his mate had left it. In the saloon the table was littered with old fish and chip papers, empty beer cans and an overflowing ashtray. One officer checked the cigarette ends. 'One roll up, the others are filters. Looks like there could have been two of them here.'

The other officer moved from the saloon into the bedroom. The double bed was unmade. On a side table was an empty coffee cup and two dog ends in a saucer. Sitting on the duvet was a dark blue holdall. 'We have a bag,' he called out then carefully unzipped it and looked inside. His colleague joined him, watching as several items of clothing were taken out: one shirt, one jersey, one pair of boxer shorts and socks plus a washbag with soap and razor. They checked the pockets of a pair of trousers for any ID. There was none.

One of the officers said, 'This bloke certainly travelled light. We'll get forensics to check everything for finger prints.'

'Do you still need me?' called Zed, who was getting cold outside.

One officer shouted, 'No, you go back son, we'll lock up.'

When he got back to the office, Zed explained. 'That bloke Colvin's gone. The boat's empty.'

Feeling foolish for being taken in Peggy said, 'So, he was involved?'

Dwain replied, 'Well if he wasn't, then it's a bit of a coincidence.'

'I knew he was a bit shifty,' Zed said. 'I mean, why would anyone hire a boat and stay in the marina?'

'I better ring Betty and let her know what's happened,' said Peggy.

They heard the chattering of the police radio before the two officers appeared in the doorway.

One said, 'Now I need you to give me a description of your guest and any other details you have on him.'

The other officer was on his radio organising the forensic team to visit the office and boat the following day.

'Well if it wasn't money then what were they after?' wondered Zed.

Now sitting on a chair at the desk, Tim recalled the discussion he and Peggy had had with Peter Baxter. 'I think I know,' he said.

Both officers looked at him. 'Why's that sir?'

After Tim's explanation the two uniformed officers became aware that this might not be a simple break in. Following a discussion one said, 'We need to report this to CID.'

Peggy still hadn't joined the dots but became horrified when realising that Quin's visit to the marina and the office break in could be to do with the death of Roy Coombs.

Dwain suddenly said, 'The poor cab driver, she's still sitting outside.'

Peggy had completely forgotten about her. 'Tell her we still need her to get home.'

'Why do you need a cab? The Land Rover's outside,' said Tim.

Peggy glared at him, growling, 'Don't you even think about driving that thing.'

Tim held his hands up. 'I was only saying.'

Dwain glanced across at Zed. 'Well, if we could drive, then we could take you home.'

'Yeah, well you know what 'if' did?' said Tim.

Innocently Zed asked, 'No, what?'

Tim was about to answer when Peggy pushed him out of the door. 'Go'.

It was two days later when DCI Bill Collins received an unexpected call from a detective inspector at Melbury CID. He listened without comment as the officer recounted the report which the two uniformed officers had passed to his department. When it was finished, he said, 'It would appear that the main suspect in this break in is a man called Quin, who we understand lives in the Sparkbrook area, on your patch.'

The DCI asked, 'You say before the break in, he booked a boat for a week in this marina?'

'He did, though under the name of Colvin.' He laughed. 'But like a numpty he left his bag behind, and guess whose fingerprints were found on it? One, Bernie Quin.'

'So, he has previous?'

'He does, spent four years inside for fraud.'
DCI Collins thought for a moment. 'Strange, burglary and violence doesn't seem his thing.'

The Melbury detective paused. 'But there's something odd about this. According to the guy who runs the marina, this break in could be connected to something bigger.'
DCI Collins asked innocently. 'Like What?'
There was an awkward silence. 'I was hoping you could tell me that Sir. You see, the 'something bigger' he referred to involves the death last year of a Roy Coombs, which is still the subject of an ongoing investigation.'

'And do you have any leads?' asked DCI Collins.
There was an embarrassed silence. 'Not yet. But it would have helped Sir, if we had known Roy Coombs was on one of your protection programmes.'

Collins hesitated before answering. 'Yes, I'm sorry about that. It was highly confidential. He already had a boat moored in that marina, so we thought it was the safest place for him to be.'

He half anticipated the DI's next cynical observation. 'Well obviously it wasn't that secure Sir.'
Collins grimaced as he spoke. 'No, and I need to find out why.'

'So where do we go with this now?' asked the local DI.

'We'll pick up this Quin character and see what he has to say. In the meantime, this is still your investigation, but there's obvious merit in us both working together on this. I was the one who assured Roy of our protection, so it runs deep with me.'

The Melbury DI agreed, and with his department's limited resources was glad of the offer from a larger force.

After ending the phone call, the DCI emailed his colleague at the National Crime Agency.

'We have local plod sniffing about in Tiddledurn. Could be a problem. Can you deal with?'

The reply came back quickly.

'We can. Is your man upstairs still obliv?'
'Yes.'
'Good, let's keep it that way.'

DCI Collins turned off his laptop and went downstairs to the squad room. His sergeant, a man younger than him, was on his third early morning cup of black coffee. He was a sturdy man from his days boxing in the Royal Navy.

The DCI laughed, 'Heavy night was it?'

Bleary eyed, the sergeant replied, 'Ladies night at the Lodge Guv.'

Collins raised his eyebrows. 'Bloody secret society.'

Over the years he had been approached many times to join the Masons but had always declined; though he often wondered if he had, whether he would have made Chief Superintendent. He had no doubt that DSU Warren Turner was also on the square, hence the early promotion.

Handing his colleague a printout he said, 'To keep the local plod in Melbury happy, we need to bring this bloke in for questioning. And he might be useful to us. All the details are on there.'

'What's it in connection with boss?' asked the sergeant.

'Believe it or not, the Roy Coombs case.'

The sergeant was surprised. 'I thought we had that tied up.'

The DCI nodded. 'So did I.

CHAPTER TWENTY

Poacher Turned Gamekeeper

Smokey Joe sat on the churchyard bench for some time, allowing the warmth of the waning afternoon sun to caress his rugged face. Even though his mind about the job offer was made up, he still felt troubled. It was if something deep inside him was wrestling with his soul, and always had been. Standing up he bade farewell to the journeyman Victor Button, then ambled slowly along the gravel path.

Occasionally he would stop to read the faded inscription on a weathered gravestone, wondering to himself. 'Where are these people now? Is there something greater after death, or just an eternal sleep, nothingness?'

Being a pragmatist and an atheist, Smokey tended to believe the latter, why would he not? Obviously, his friend in the Manse believed in eschatology or he wouldn't be doing that job. Or was he himself too disillusioned. He thought that maybe he would only rid himself of this hollowness when he was also buried underneath the sod.

A young couple holding a bunch of flowers came through the gate from the lane. Ahead of them ran a small girl no more than five or six years of age. Her bright pink tee shirt and shoes contrasted vividly with the drabness of the burial ground. As she ran towards Smokey he was enchanted by her carefree and happy demeanour, thinking, 'As a child I must have been like that once.'

Suddenly she stopped, being aware of the tall figure with his wide brimmed hat with a long pheasant's feather and bushy beard. Smokey smiled,

'Hello, what's your name?'

Turning firstly to her parents for reassurance she answered softly, 'It's Lucy.'

'That's a very pretty name.'

'That's a big feather in your hat.'

Smokey took it off, then bending down showed it to her. 'It's a pheasant's feather.'

'What's a pheasant?' she asked.

Having caught up with her, her mother said, 'I Hope she's not bothering you.'

Smokey smiled. 'On the contrary, it's nice to meet such a bright young thing.'

'We've come to put some flowers on my father's grave,' said her husband. 'He died suddenly last year. Lucy was very fond of him, and we've struggled to explain to her what had happened.'

Smokey nodded. 'I can understand that.'

The father continued. 'But now she believes that his spirit is in heaven with the angels and the grave only contains his body.'

Smokey said, 'That's very nice.'

After leaving the happy little family he left the churchyard and went out into the lane. As he walked towards the Manse he said aloud, 'Driftwood, I hope you're right about this my old mate.'

On reaching the gate, he stood for a moment before going in. Then pushing it open went up the weed infested path. He banged on the heavy oak door and waited. The vicar's friendly wife opened it, her hands covered in flour.

'Oh, hello, Joe, come in. He's in the garden, I'll call him.'

Joe went through to the spacious, cluttered sitting room. She called from the kitchen, 'take a seat and I'll put the kettle on.'

Minutes later the vicar, his face red with exertion, appeared wearing a black apron and holding a pair of secateurs. 'Hello Joe, just been doing a bit of pruning.

The garden is an overgrown jungle. Too much for us really but we try to keep on top of it.'

His wife came from the kitchen and set a tray on a small table. 'I'll leave you two to it,' she said disappearing back to the kitchen.

Smokey Joe smiled. 'That's lovely thanks.'

The vicar sat down opposite Smokey then asked, 'So, Joe, have you decided?'

Smokey Joe nodded. 'I have, yes.'

'And what is the answer?' asked the vicar as he was pouring the tea.

Smokey took a deep breath. 'I'll go for it.'

The vicar grinned. 'I am so pleased Joe. I know it's been a difficult decision, but I'm sure it's for the best.'

'So, what happens now?' asked Smokey.

The vicar dunked a biscuit into his tea. 'Well, I will arrange for you to meet the estate manager, but that is only a formality. They know all about you and are looking forward to meeting you. In a small community like this my recommendation goes a long way.'

Smokey laughed. 'Well, I'm very grateful, but I hope you don't expect me to attend church on Sunday.'

The vicar held up his hands. 'No pressure Joe, I promise.' He chuckled. 'Though God works in mysterious ways. Now let's celebrate with something a little stronger.'

The following morning Smokey crawled from his tent. His eyes squinted painfully at the bright daylight and his head felt as if it had been hit by a mallet. The previous night the vicar's wife had insisted he stayed to dinner, then afterwards he and the clergyman had demolished a bottle of single malt whisky. He groaned. 'I can't drink like I used to.' Reaching for a bucket he filled it with cold water and dunked his head into it. A voice as fresh and loud as the dawn chorus called out. 'Good morning, Joe.' Lifting his head from the bucket he saw the vicar standing feet away. 'Oh dear you seem a bit worse for wear my friend.'

Smokey shook his head then asked, 'How do you do it?'

The vicar laughed. 'I've got many more miles on the clock than you, and I think my liver's given up complaining. Why don't you come to the Manse for some black coffee and sober up. The estate manager is coming to see you this afternoon.'

Again, Smokey groaned. 'Oh, great he'll think I'm a bloody drunk.'

Before going across to the Manse, he stripped off and washed himself from head to toe. There was little chance of anybody seeing his naked body, unless of course the vicar's wife was looking out of a window. He chuckled at the thought, 'Something to excite the ladies at the Women's Institute meeting!'

After dressing in clean clothes, he took out his mobile phone. There was one more person he had to tell of his decision. He tapped in Tim's number. Tim sounded weary when he answered, and it soon became clear to Smokey why. He was outraged when told of the break in at the marina, and subsequent violent assault on his friend. Smokey used many expletives in relation to the perpetrators and indicated fervently what type of retribution he would afflict upon them given the opportunity.

Eventually Smokey told Tim of his good fortune. At first, he was shocked and surprised, but as Smokey explained the circumstances, he agreed it was a good move, though they would of course miss him. Smokey had laughed saying 'It's only in Abbotsbury, not Australia.'

Simultaneously the bell on the church tower and the grandfather clock in the hall of the Manse struck two. Smokey Joe nervously twiddled his long beard. There was a knock on the front door. The vicar jumped up. 'Right on time.'

Smokey Joe waited whilst he left the room to let the estate manager in. He chided himself for feeling so anxious, although it was the first time he had been interviewed for a job since joining the army many years before. Hearing voices in the hallway he stood up.

The vicar, all smiles, said, 'Joe, this is Laura, the estate manager.'

For a moment he was tongue tied. He was expecting the estate manager to be a man, maybe fifties, portly with rugged face and dressed in tweeds; not a slim, attractive, middle aged woman in jeans. She held out her hand.

'Good to meet you Joe, I've heard a lot about you.' Looking at the vicar Smokey winked. 'All good I hope.'

'Please do sit down,' said the vicar. As if on cue his kindly wife appeared with tea and freshly made scones, then as usual vanished to another room.

As interviews go it was laced with anecdotes, memories and laughter. Laura found it particularly amusing that he had been a poacher.

When he asked who the gamekeeper was that he would be assisting, she hesitated before answering. 'It's me. I'm afraid I'm both for the time being.'

Anticipating Smokey's surprise, she explained. 'It used to be my husband, but sadly we lost him last year in a road accident.'

Having lost close friends himself Smokey Joe could recognise the pain in her eyes. 'I'm so sorry.'

She shrugged and smiled. 'Thank you Joe.'

He instinctively wanted to give her a hug.

The vicar said, 'I didn't think it appropriate to mention it before.'

The clock in the hallway struck four.

'Good grief,' said Laura. 'Is that the time? I must be going. The children will be home.'

As she stood, the vicar asked, 'So, will he do?'

Laura laughed. 'Very well indeed.' She held out her hand, 'Welcome to Illchester Estates Joe. Come by tomorrow, and I'll show you round and of course the location of your cottage.'

'I'll drive him up,' the vicar volunteered.

She smiled. 'Good idea.' Then hesitating added, 'I forgot to ask Joe, 'You do drive?'

Smokey laughed. 'Anything from jeeps to tanks, though not for some time.'

Disappearing along the hall she called out, 'Good, we haven't got any tanks but there's a Land Rover that goes with the job.'

As she left the house a waft of scented perfume lingered heavily in the air.

CHAPTER TWENTY ONE

The Reluctant Informer

Arriving on the outskirts of Birmingham, Beaky Quin dropped his safe breaking mate off at a bus station in Solihull, for his onward journey to Coventry. Driving towards Sparkbrook he worried how he would explain to Jimmy Doyle about the failed break in at the marina. As far as he knew Jimmy distanced himself from the day to day criminal activities of Duncan Hicks and Sahil Ali. The Blue Diamond club though was a go to hangout for the gang and Jimmy was a loyal friend of theirs. There was a rumour that, when living in Belfast he had been involved with the IRA, so he was not a man to be crossed.

Beaky's small, first floor flat next to the launderette was as equally untidy and disorganised as his office below. Beaky hadn't slept well that night. All he could think about was the bag which he had stupidly left on the hire boat 'Moorhen' and whether it could be traced to him.

He had his answer early the next morning. As first light began to illuminate the interior of the small bedroom a knock, loud and purposeful, struck the front door. Sleepily Beaky stepped from the bed and pulled back the curtains. Standing on the pavement below were two men, their car parked alongside the kerb. Beaky's stomach lurched. Again, a loud knock followed by a shout, 'Open up, it's the police.'

For a moment he considered staying quiet and hiding, but what was the point, they would only come back later, or worse force entry. Reluctantly accepting the inevitable he threw on his dressing gown and went downstairs. As he unlocked and opened the door one of the men produced a police warrant card.

'Are you Mark Quin?'

Beaky nodded, 'I am.'

'Mr Quin you are under arrest on suspicion of burglary and assault.' Beaky remained silent. What could he say? If they had found his fingerprints on the bag, he was banged to rights. After cautioning him they accompanied him upstairs to get dressed.

Beaky stared from the back seat of the unmarked police car as his home turf flashed by. Having lived most of his life in Sparkbrook he knew the route to the police station, and this was not it. Nervously he asked, 'Where are we going?'
From the front passenger seat the sergeant said, 'Don't worry about that Mr Quin, we'll be there shortly.'

Again, his stomach lurched, were these really police, or people sent by Jimmy Doyle? Either way it wasn't good. On the outskirts of Sparkbrook, they turned off the main road into a small trading estate, stopping outside a detached building advertising computer technology.

'Where are we?' asked Beaky.
The sergeant didn't answer, instead saying curtly, 'Out.'
Inside they passed through an open plan office with six unoccupied desks. A door at the end led to a small windowless room. In the middle was a square wooden table and four chairs. The sergeant told him gruffly to sit down. Submissively Beaky did as he was asked. The sergeant then left the room locking the door behind him.

In despair Beaky stared at the four cream coloured walls, thinking 'what was this place and who were these people?' His mind raced as he considered which would be worse, to be charged and a possible prison sentence or face Jimmy Doyle's wrath. Should Jimmy hear that he had been arrested then he might worry he'd be implicated. Not that Beaky would ever grass, but Jimmy wouldn't take that chance. He shuddered at the thought of what he might do.

Shortly afterwards the door opened, and a man came in accompanied by a stony face woman. They both sat down opposite Beaky. The man turned on a recording machine, introducing himself as DCI Collins. The female detective remained silent. The DCI placed a buff coloured folder on the table. For a moment he said nothing, just stared across the table at Beaky, as if trying to get the measure of the little man. This face to face scrutiny made Beaky feel even more anxious than he already was.

The DCI smiled, 'Right Mr Quin, we'll keep this brief. We know you were involved in the break in and an assault at the marina in Tiddledurn, so there's no point in denying it.' This was a bit of a bluff, which the DCI hoped would nudge him in the right direction. For although his fingerprints had been found on the bag in the hire boat, there was no actual forensic evidence linking him to the crimes in the office. The DCI continued his questioning.

'Why did you travel all that way? What were you after? Clearly not money.'

Beaky replied, 'no comment.'

'Did you have an accomplice, and if so who?'

'No comment.'

'We know you are a private eye. Did someone hire you to break in?'

'No comment.'

The female officer took over. 'We believe that you regularly frequent the Blue Diamond Club, is that right?'

Beaky Quin nodded.

She continued, 'And you are acquainted with the owner, Jimmy Doyle?'

The mention of this name provoked a flicker of panic in his eyes.

Picking up on this, the DCI asked, 'Did he put you up to this?'

Feeling distinctly uncomfortable, again Beaky answered. 'No comment.'

After glancing at each other the two detectives stood up. The DCI turned off the recording machine. 'We'll take a break there, Mr Quin.'

They both left Beaky alone in the stuffy room. It reminded him of his cell in prison on a hot day. The thought of returning there made him shiver. Now he wondered what the hell he had got himself into. Eventually after what seemed an age the two detectives returned. Again, they sat down opposite Beaky. This time the recording machine was not switched on.

The DCI started, 'Right Mr Quin, you can cut the 'no comment' bullshit. We've got you bang to rights. So, you have two choices. You can either help us, or we charge you with burglary and assault and you go down.'

Beaky looked up from the desk. 'How do you mean, help you?'

The female detective continued, 'We want you to feed back to us as much information as you can about Jimmy Doyle and the Blue Diamond club. We know it's also used as a base by known criminals.'

Beaky's stomach was churning and he could feel the sweat forming on his forehead.

'So, what's it to be then?' the DCI asked impatiently.

Beaky quickly computed his limited options. He couldn't go back to prison. He was not a strong man and it had nearly destroyed him last time. On the other hand, if Jimmy Doyle found out he was passing information to the police he would be a dead man.

Jokingly the DCI asked, 'Do you want to phone a friend?'

Beaky was not amused. 'I'm stuffed either way, aren't I?'

It had been three days since the break in at the marina. Whilst not admitting it, Tim was still feeling the effects of the attack on him. Peggy had insisted he stay at the cottage and rest. This had done nothing to improve his mood which fluctuated between frustration and anger. That morning Zed, Dwain and Peggy had left for the marina, leaving Tim kicking his heels in boredom. Although once out of sight he was grateful for the opportunity to have a sleep on the sofa.

The office door had been repaired, but the mess inside was just as Beaky Quin and his mate had left it. Particles of a white dust like substance were in evidence where the forensic officers had been searching for fingerprints and other evidence. Looking around, Peggy despaired at the numerous scattered files thrown from the cabinet onto the floor. She sighed. 'This will take an age to sort out.'

There was a knock at the door and a boater asked. 'Are you open today? I need some fuel.'
Before Peggy had time to react angrily Dwain said, 'I'll sort it.'
Whilst Dwain was filling the boater's fuel tank Zed walked across to the hire boat 'Moorhen'. As with the office, the interior of the small boat was just as the two men and forensic officers had left it.

Unlike Dwain, Zed was a placid individual, but as he looked around the boat and thought about the attack on Tim, he felt the unusual emotion of anger rising within him. He decided to take the boat across to the service point so he and Dwain could clean it up. After starting the engine, he released the bow and stern lines and pushed off from the pontoon. Keeping to a low speed, the boat drifted slowly astern. Pushing the gear forward, he leant on the tiller bar and headed into the middle of the marina.

As the boater was still on the service jetty, he put 'Moorhen' into neutral gear, allowing it to drift gently on the afternoon breeze. Against a backdrop of a pale blue wispy sky, a kestrel hovered effortlessly on thermal air.

The scenic silence broken only by the occasional quacking ducks or squawking Canada geese. Breathing in the sweet smelling country air he thought how much he loved this place and could never imagine living anywhere else.

A tear welled in his eye as he remembered his mum. She would have been so happy here. But unlike him and Dwain she hadn't been able to escape the malign clutches of the Rotherhithe housing estate and the drug dealers. Now, at such a young age, she was gone and what could have been, was now only a distant memory.

Lost in thought, he didn't hear Dwain shout to him from the service quay. 'Come on Zed, he's finished.' As the boater moved away, Zed nudged the throttle and went alongside. Dwain took hold of the mid line and secured the boat around a bollard.

Seeing them both outside, Peggy called from the office. 'Tim's just phoned, you'll never guess what he told me?'

Dwain joked. 'Blimey he's going to give us a pay rise.'

'It must have been that bang on the head,' said Zed.

Peggy had made good progress with the discarded files, though there was still much to do. She made herself a cup of tea and put two cans of cola on the desk.

'So, we're all ears,' said Dwain.

Peggy laughed. 'Tim had a phone call from Smokey Joe, and guess what?'

The boys shrugged.

Peggy continued. 'He's taken a full time job as a gamekeeper in Abbotsbury.'

Astonished, the boys looked at each other then burst out laughing.

'But he's a poacher,' said Zed.

Peggy grinned. 'Well sometimes it takes a thief to catch a thief.'

'So where is Abbotsbury?' asked Dwain.

'It's not far from here,' replied Peggy.

Zed took a swig from the can. 'Oh, that's good we can go and visit him.'

'You could. Apparently he's also been given a cottage to live in. The old devil's really fallen on his feet.'

CHAPTER TWENTY TWO

Fraying Nerves

There were two men, both at opposite ends of the criminal spectrum who were growing increasingly impatient. The Blue Diamond club owner Jimmy Doyle, who was yet to hear from Beaky Quin who had been at the marina now for three days and there had been no communication. Jimmy's growing irritation was being further fuelled by pressure from Duncan Hicks and Sahil Ali, who were phoning him regularly from Winson Green prison.

Hicks, in particular who had psychopathic traits, was becoming more agitated, screaming obscenities and threats to Doyle. Both men were desperate to know about the elimination of any people or new evidence that could return them to prison for a long time. Whilst Doyle could reason with Ali it was impossible with Hicks.

It was Friday night in the Blue Diamond Club and it was as usual heaving. The regular punters were mostly villains and local wheeler dealers. A few of them had flashily dressed and made up young women hanging on their arms. On the small brightly lit stage three scantily dressed women were gyrating to 'Pour It Up' by Rhianna. Occasionally they would throw an item of clothing into the hands of the lecherous audience. Grown men would fight each other to catch the discarded sweaty garment.

Jimmy Doyle sat at the bar savouring his third whisky of the evening. Hick's violent threats had got under his skin. Not that he was afraid of him, but his irrational behaviour could prove dangerous to them all. He needed information and he needed it fast. Against his better instincts he took out his mobile and phoned his contact at Sparkbrook Police Station.

At first it went to answer phone. He waited for the message to end then tapped in the number again. A guarded voice answered, 'Hello.'

Jimmy growled. 'It's me.'

The reply was anxious and curt. 'What the hell are you doing phoning me on this number.'

Doyle ignored the outburst. 'I need to know what's going on. Hicks and Ali are getting pissed off.'

His contact quietly replied. 'Tell them to stop worrying. As far as we're concerned there's no further evidence against them.'

'I bloody hope so, for your sake,' said Doyle.

The phone went dead.

Detective Superintendent Turner's heart was pounding and his hands were shaking. Placing the phone back into his pocket he rued the day he ever got involved with Jimmy Doyle and his mates; but there had been little choice. The gambling had started as a younger man. The odd bet on the horses, late night card games with friends, all fairly low key stuff.

It was after his transfer to Sparkbrook Police Station as a Detective Inspector, when a few colleagues who, unbeknown to him were in the pay of Jimmy Doyle, offered to take him to a local club. He remembered their reassuring words even now. 'It's all above board Guv. You get a few of the local villains in, but that's not a bad thing for picking up info.' So being a new boy to the patch and keen to integrate with the team he went.

The trap was well set and after a few double vodka's, courtesy of the house, a pretty female hostess guided him gently towards the gambling tables. The old bug which had been dormant for many years returned, its appetite for winning more insatiable than ever. So, over the following year he became a regular visitor to the Blue Diamond Club, always telling his wife that he was working late. Of course, Jimmy Doyle happily facilitated this addiction ensuring he always had enough credit to continue playing.

The sting came late one night when Jimmy Doyle asked him to come into his office. 'Have a seat Warren.' He pointed to a chair on the opposite side of his desk. After pouring two large whiskies he said, 'I'm afraid we have a little problem mate.' Sliding a piece of paper across the surface of the desk, he watched carefully as Warren Turner picked it up and absorbed the large amount written down. His wide, unblinking eyes and open mouth a precursor to panic.

Jimmy smiled. 'That's right, I'm afraid that's the amount you owe the house.' Then holding up his hands in a friendly gesture, he said, 'Look mate, we're all friends here, don't worry about it. I'm sure we can come to some arrangement that will be beneficial to us both.'

Doyle glanced around the club, every table was now full. The electronic gaming machines and illegal poker and crap tables were all doing good business. It was a large square space with a low, nicotine stained ceiling. The entrance was at the far end, which Jimmy could see over the heads of the customers. He had just asked the barmen to top his whisky up when the unmistakable, gaunt figure of Beaky Quin came through the door.

Pushing through the throng he made his way to where Jimmy Doyle was sitting. 'Where the hell have you been?'
Defensively Beaky replied, 'You said I had a week.'
Jimmy's eyes bored into him. 'I told you the bloody boat was booked for a week. It doesn't take that long to get a result.' Jumping down off the stool he told Beaky to follow him.

In Jimmy's office Beaky sat in a chair by his desk. Jimmy, standing menacingly in front of him, lit a cigar, blowing the smoke in Beaky's direction. 'So, what have we got?'

Over the next few minutes, he listened with growing incredulity as Beaky nervously relayed the story of the ill- fated break in at the marina. Occasionally he paused as his mouth dried like a sun drenched pool. His weak stomach churned as he contemplated the choice given to him by DCI Collins. He had chosen the one which maintained his freedom, and now he had to deliver.

Jimmy Doyle shook his head in despair. 'You total bloody idiot! A simple job and you balls it up. Call yourself a private eye.'

Beaky protested, 'But what else could we do? What if the bloke came round?'

Jimmy drew close to his face. Beaky could smell the whisky on his breath. He shouted, 'You should have belted him again, then carried on searching, not cleared off like a couple of losers.' He then walked around his desk and sat down. 'I just hope for your sake that fuck up can't be traced back to us.'

Beaky's hands and knees were trembling. He dreaded Jimmy finding out about the forgotten bag and his arrest. He stuttered. 'I...I... I'm really sorry Jimmy, what more can I say?'

Exasperated with his pathetic excuses Jimmy told him to get out.

As Beaky stood up Jimmy added, 'And don't think you're getting paid for that balls up.'

At the bar Beaky ordered a double brandy. The barmen said sympathetically, 'You look a bit rough mate.'

Beaky shook his head. 'Don't ask.'

He found a table in the corner and sat down. It had been a long day and the brandy only enhanced his tiredness. Closing his eyes he thought to himself. 'How the hell am I going to find out anything about Jimmy Doyle's activities?'

As well as acting as an intermediary for Hicks and Ali, Jimmy had his own concerns. He regretted the day that they had persuaded him to do their bidding. If his involvement was discovered, it would put him behind bars for a long time. As conversations could be overheard, using the prison phone was not an option. This deadly request had been relayed to him via their bent lawyer. In Belfast he had been the go to person for such things, but that was all behind him, or so he thought. Considering his options he lit another cigar and blew a cloud of grey smoke towards the office ceiling. He closed his eyes thinking.

'This bloody Roy Coombs file is haunting me.' Although he knew there was the possibility that, like Roy Coombs, it had perished in the fire. Hicks and Ali, clearly believed it still existed, and their paranoia could not be pacified until it was found. Beaky Quin's failure had burned that bridge, so in the absence of anything else there was one man who might know more than he was saying, Peter Baxter. Maybe it was time for a face to face discussion with the bookie.

Peter Baxter knew the prison release date for Hicks and Ali was getting closer. Without new and substantive evidence, they would soon be back on the streets terrorising local retailers for protection money. How could he tell his two friends, the Indian restaurant owner Amit Thakur and publican Gerry Carter that he had inadvertently stumbled into a covert police operation.

This National Crime Agency operation regarded their personal concerns as just one part of a major investigation into more serious widespread crimes. He needed to make his friends understand that he trusted an honest copper who was not in the pockets of Hick and Ali.

Having had a sleepless night, he left his home early and walked along Sparkbrook High Street towards his bookmaker's shop. The demise of this once thriving retail centre, now full of charity shops, nail bars and Turkish barbers depressed him. Clouds of toxic fumes spewed from the stationary cars waiting at the traffic lights. He despaired of the zombie like people fixated on their phones with little regard for anyone walking towards them.

On reaching the shop he unlocked the door and quickly went in to disarm the alarm. At least he remembered the code this time. The staff wouldn't arrive for at least another hour which would give him time to check his Facebook and Whatsapp accounts. He had just opened his laptop when a loud knock on the front door shook him from his calm repose. Irritated, he stood up and went from his office into the shop. He gestured to the two men. 'We're not open yet.' They both stood there glaring at him through the glass.

Again, he repeated, 'We're not open.' This time one of them produced a short crow bar and went to smash the window. Peter Baxter froze. 'Alright, alright.' As he unlocked the door both men pushed their way inside the shop.

Baxter took a defensive step backwards as their intimidating presence confronted him. The one with the gold cross hanging from his ear said, 'There's someone who wants to talk to you mate.'

Meekly Baxter asked, 'Who and why?'

The other, whose size and flat nose resembled that of a veteran boxer grabbed his arm, 'Don't worry about that pal.' There was no point in struggling, his grip was vice like.

Parked outside against the kerb was a silver Nissan. The back door was opened and Baxter shoved roughly in. His flat nosed man handler moved in beside him. As the car sped off through the streets of

Sparkbrook Peter Baxter feared this could be the 'mafia moment' he had fantasised about. Taken to a disused warehouse, tortured for information then shot in the head. This macabre thought sent shivers along his spine.

After passing through the centre of Birmingham they turned into a road adjacent to New Street Station. This was a seedy part of the city which he had never needed or wanted to frequent. The car drew to a stop outside the back entrance to the Blue Diamond Club. As his flat nosed companion jumped out, he noticed a tattoo of a roaring lion on his thick neck.

He beckoned to Baxter to follow him. His partner walked behind. Passing a bare room stacked high with beer crates and barrels they went through a door into the main club area. Having no windows and the lights dimmed it gave the eerie appearance of an underground cave. The smell of stale beer was overwhelming.

Peter breathed a slight sigh of relief; at least it wasn't a disused warehouse on some run down industrial estate. From behind the bar a voice deep with an Ulster dialect called. 'Bring him in here.'

CHAPTER TWENTY THREE

She's Leaving Home

A warm breeze blew across the canal from the open fields beyond. Rocket Ron was returning from his usual evening walk along the towpath,_regularly he would go as far as Muckle Farm. The now derelict buildings and his and Rose's old moorings were full of fond memories. He often_thought that on ageing, new experiences become limited, leaving only distorted recollections of the past.

His two ferrets, Frankie and Freddie, scampered along in front of him. Whilst not everyone's idea of a pet, they had been his constant companions for a long time. But like him they were getting older and slower. He knew their average life span was between five and ten years and the thought of losing them filled him full of dread.

His was one of three narrowboats moored on this stretch of the canal. The other two were occupied by Zed and Dwain. For years Rocket Ron was moored alongside his friend, the mildly eccentric herbalist Rose. Following deteriorating health, she had decided to sell her boat and move into sheltered accommodation in Melbury town. Ron was bereft at being left on his own, so Tim arranged for him to move his boat near to his cottage and alongside Zed and Dwain.

He was in a world of his own as he sauntered along. As happiness went, it was the best he could hope for, and he was grateful for it. Although they hadn't walked far, Freddie and Frankie's pace was slowing. Several times he nearly tripped as they got close to his feet. He shouted at them both. 'Get on with you, wretched rodents.' They ran ahead of him, though not too far.

Nearing his boat, he stood for a moment listening to the birdsong and whispering of the leaves as the breeze shook their branches.

The voice ahead startled him. 'Hello Ron.'

Briefly he struggled to recognise the young teenage girl standing next to Dwain's boat.

She called out to him, 'It's Phoebe, Ron.'

Drawing closer he remembered her from the bonfire they were previously sitting around in the field. He joked. 'Sorry I really must go to the opticians.'

She smiled nervously as Frankie and Freddie encircled her. Ron poked them both with his stick. 'Get away you two.' They quickly scampered off up a nearby bank.

'Sorry to disturb you,' she said. 'I was looking for Dwain. I've been trying his mobile but it's going straight to answer phone.'

Ron could tell from her red watery eyes that she had been crying. 'What's up Phoebe? Are you ok?'

Her trembling lip was the prelude to a flood of tears.

'I've left home,' she sobbed, 'and I'm not going back.'

Ron, a lifelong bachelor, was ill equipped to deal with this hormonal teenage emotion.

'Look Phoebe love, Dwain's not here. Why don't you come on my boat and tell me all about it.'

She wiped her eyes with a tissue and nodded. 'If that's ok, thanks.'

Frankie and Freddie followed them in then settled down in their usual place on the carpet by the stove. Ron picked up the kettle. 'Sit yourself down love and I'll make a nice cuppa.'

'Do you know what time Dwain comes back?' she asked.

Ron took two mugs from the cupboard. 'I don't my dear. It could be anytime. Now let's make the brew then you can tell me what's happened.'

Phoebe's mobile rang. She took it from her pocket, glanced at it and turned it off. Ron guessed it was her mother but said nothing.

He put the two mugs and a packet of biscuits on a small round table then sat down opposite her. 'Now Phoebe, what's going on?'

Taking a sip of the tea, she said, 'I'm nearly eighteen and my mum still treats me as if I was ten. After I got back from school, we had a big row and I walked out.'

Ron subtly observed, 'And was this anything to do with Dwain? You both seemed very close at the bonfire.'

Phoebe nodded. 'It's just not fair. George is allowed to stay overnight with Zed, but I'm not allowed to with Dwain.'

Not knowing of the boys' intimate relationship, Ron answered pragmatically, 'Well there is a bit of a difference Phoebe. I can see your mum's point.'

This was not the answer Phoebe wanted.

She flared. 'Just because they are two boys doesn't mean they don't…'

Suddenly she stopped realising too much had been said. Ron though had got the gist of her outburst.

He smiled, 'Oh, I see.'

'All she's worried about is me getting pregnant and not going to university.'

'Your mum will be worried where you are, why not ring her?'

Indifferent to his request, she replied, 'Let her worry, it's all her fault anyway.'

Ron soon realised that this was way beyond his meagre mediation skills.

'Tell you what Phoebe, you stay here. I'll walk down to the cottage and see if Dwain is there. How's that?'

Sullenly, she nodded. 'Ok Ron. Thanks.'

The boys and Peggy had not long returned from the marina. Zed was surprised that his Gran wasn't there, she would normally be cooking the evening meal for them all. Tim had swapped the sofa for his armchair by the fireplace. A faint gurgling snore came from his open mouth.

'Look at him,' said Zed. 'I thought he didn't like resting.'

Tim stirred and one eye slowly opened. 'Did someone mention a brew?'

Dwain laughed. 'I'll do it.'

Tim yawned and stretched. 'Oh, Betty rang. She's not feeling too good, bit of breathlessness.'

Concerned for her Peggy said, 'I'll, ring her now.'

There was a sudden loud knock on the door. Zed, who was taking off his overalls and boots, opened it. Frankie and Freddie darted between his legs into the sitting room.

Ron shouted at them, 'Come 'ere you bloody rodents.'

Both the animals took no notice and made straight for where Tim was sitting. They knew he always gave them a treat. Tim called to Dwain in the kitchen. 'Bring in a couple of bacon bits lad.'

Ron shook his head. 'They think they're dogs.'

'So, to what do we owe the pleasure my friend?' asked Tim.

Sitting down on the sofa, Ron replied, 'It's Dwain I've come to see.'

Hearing his name Dwain came from the kitchen holding two mugs of tea.

'What's up Ron?' he asked.

Ron took a mouthful of the hot brew. 'I've got Phoebe on my boat. She was looking for you.'

Surprised, Dwain asked, 'Why, is she alright?'

'Apparently she's run away from home.'

'What?' yelled Dwain. 'Her mother will go mental. I'd better go and see what's going on.'

161

Ron nodded. 'Good idea son.'

Tim shook his head in despair, 'Teenagers!'

Peggy had more important things concerning her. 'Betty's not answering. I've tried three times and it keeps going to answerphone.'

'Well, she did sound pretty rough when she called. Maybe she's gone to bed early,' replied Tim.

'No, that's not like her. I'm going over there.'

Forgetting that the Land Rover was still at the marina, Tim offered to take her to Betty's flat in Tiddledurn. Peggy curtly reminded him then added sharply, 'Someone else in this family needs to be able to drive. It's ridiculous. I'll phone a cab.'

'I'll come with you,' said Zed.

Following up Peggy's loaded observation, Ron asked, 'Aren't the two boys old enough to hold a provisional licence now?'

Tim nodded. 'They are, God help the other road users.'

Peter Baxter sat in Jimmy Doyle's office occupying the same chair as Beaky Quin had the previous evening. He had no idea where they had brought him to, although it was clearly some sort of club. Peter noted his inquisitor was well built, early fifties with a strong Northern Irish accent. He had a broad brow which made his dark eyes seem as if they were deeper set than they were.

Unlike with Beaky, Jimmy offered him an alcoholic drink. He refused, after all it was only ten in the morning. Jimmy suggested a coffee might be preferable. As anxiety had rendered his mouth like sandpaper, Peter nodded. 'Thanks, black no sugar.'

One of the heavies guarded the office door as if anticipating an attempted escape. This was the last thing on Peter Baxter's mind. He thought a baseball bat, or worse a bullet in the head, was still a possibility. Jimmy Doyle pulled a chair up alongside him. There was a strong smell of a heavily scented after shave. Jimmy smiled.

'Now Mr Baxter we have a little problem. It seems we both have an interest in this file which Roy Coombs has apparently compiled on my friends Hicks and Ali.'

What could he say? It was obvious that this character knew of his recent enquiries. The other heavy arrived with a whisky for Jimmy and a coffee for Peter. Jimmy continued. 'I also understand that you were....' He chuckled before continuing, 'part of their business activities.'

Peter Baxter bit hard on this glib remark. 'If you are referring to me and my friends being victims of their bloody protection racket, then yes.'

Jimmy said, 'Yeah, that's unfortunate. But I'm not part of that.'

He took a deep breath and bravely asked, 'So why are you interested in them?'

Jimmy lit a cigar and laughed. 'Let's just say from time to time they help keep my beak wet.' The heavy guarding the door also laughed.

'So, what do you want from me?' asked Peter.

Jimmy took a sip of his whisky. 'It's very simple. I want you to tell me all you have discovered about this file.'

Peter Baxter laughed nervously. 'Well, that won't take long. I haven't found it.'

Jimmy blew another cloud of smoke upwards. 'And how about your friend DCI Collins at Sparkbrook nick?'

This unexpected remark threw Peter. How the hell did he know about that he wondered. This reaction was not lost on Jimmy Doyle.

He grinned. 'Oh yes, we know about that too. So while you're at it you can tell me about your conversations with him.'

Stupidly Peter asked, 'Like what?'

Swiftly Jimmy dropped the easy going manner. Thumping the desk with his fist he shouted, 'Like what else the old bill are looking into.'

This loud outburst unsettled Peter and any bravado he had previously mustered disappeared like a burst bubble.

He stuttered. 'How would I know? They wouldn't confide in me. All we talked about was Roy Coombs and the file.' Peter was never good at lying and could feel the blood pumping on his cheeks.

Jimmy swigged back the remainder of his whisky. He smiled sceptically. 'So you say Mr Baxter. So you say. The question is, do I believe you?'

CHAPTER TWENTY FOUR

The Net Tightens

It had been a little while since DCI Collins had interviewed Beaky Quin. He had not long arrived in his office at Sparkbrook Police Station when the call from his colleague at the National Crime Agency came through. There was a hint of delight in her voice. 'There has been contact with your man upstairs and we have a transcript of the call.'

'Well done,' said the DCI. 'They must be starting to panic.'

'The call was traced to the mobile of Jimmy Doyle.'

The DCI chuckled. 'Well, well, the owner of the Blue Diamond Club.'

'We did some background checks on our Mr Doyle. He did time at the Maze prison in Northern Ireland, for guess what?'

The DCI needed no prompting. 'Dabbling in explosives?'

She laughed. 'More than dabbling Bill. Apparently, he was the go to man when it came to making and planting.'

Bill Collins said, ''I've got a regular attendee at the club. He's feeding me back information, but I don't hold out too much hope.'

The NCA detective was not so sure. 'We now need anything that can link Doyle to the explosion at the marina. You may need to turn your snout's screws.'

'How are the drugs team doing?' asked Collins.

He imagined her smiling contentedly. 'They've been putting pressure on the street dealers. Their supplies all link back to Hicks and Ali. The Roy Coombs file gave us some credible information to go on. He really did his homework.'

The DCI smiled. 'I'll tell him.'

'Can you really speak with ghosts Bill?'

'Have you had any kickback on the John Doe?' he asked.

The answer was nonchalant, 'No, and never will. He was just another faceless junky.'

After finishing the call, DCI Bill Collins walked along the passage to the coffee machine. Selected a strong white, kicked the base and waited. As the brown liquid slowly dribbled into the plastic cup he reflected on his colleague's words. She was right, they had to find something linking Jimmy Doyle to the explosion. His back history and connection to Hicks and Ali was too much of a coincidence to ignore. Proving it though was a different ball game.

Back in his office, he pushed aside some papers, placed his coffee on the desk and leant back in his chair, saying out loud, 'Someone in that club must know something.' It was time to pressure Beaky Quin. He picked up the phone and called the squad room one floor below.

His sergeant answered. 'Yes Guv.'

'It's time we had another chat with Beaky Quin, go fetch him.'

'And take him to the same location as before?'

'Yes,' said the DCI, 'we don't want eyes on him here at the nick. I'll clear it with the NCA, it's their place.'

Unbeknown to DCI Collins, Beaky Quin had made some progress with his task. Spurred on by fear of the alternative, he knew feeding back something, albeit a few crumbs to the police could keep him from being charged and a possible prison sentence.

At the Blue Diamond Club, he had befriended a new and lonely young barman of Romanian descent. It immediately struck Beaky that with the lad's good English he was someone he could use. After his shift had finished he and Beaky would drink and talk into the early hours. It soon became apparent that he was not on these shores legally and was desperate not to be deported.

Beaky had suggested that he knew people who might be able to support his asylum claim. But there would be a price. Helplessly, the lad had held up his hands. 'But I have no money.'

Beaky had laughed. 'It's not money I need mate.'

The barman listened as Beaky laid out his requirements. 'All I need you to do is keep your eyes and ears open. Pay particular attention to the conversations of Doyle's two heavies. They're always in here getting pissed and shouting their mouths off. They're more likely to spill something than Doyle.'

The poor lad was mortified at the suggestion. 'What if I get caught?'

'Of course it's a risk. But you don't need to write anything down.' He pointed to his head. 'Just keep it all in there and tell me when we meet.'

The lad asked, 'And you say this could help me to stay in England?'

Beaky nodded. 'It will certainly go in your favour with the people I know.'

This was of course untrue. But if it gave him some leverage then so be it.

Dwain had run all the way from the cottage to Ron's boat. He knew Phoebe's mother. Lady Barrington Gore, would blame him for Phoebe's tempestuous behaviour. Whilst she tolerated their teenage relationship, it was obvious she thought her daughter could do better than him. No doubt hoping that when at university, she would meet someone more suitable.

When he arrived at Ron's boat, Phoebe threw her arms around him sobbing. 'I've been trying to get hold of you.'

Gently he sat her down on the two seat sofa. 'Ron told me what's happened Phoebe, you can't just leave home. What were you thinking?'

She blinked back tears. 'I'm not going back there. I want to live here with you.'

Sitting down next to her, he said, 'That's cool Pheebs, but it's impossible. You know that.'

Her long hair was flicked away from her damp cheeks. 'So, you don't want me to stay here then?'

He took hold of her hand. 'Of course I do. But be realistic it's not going to happen. What about Uni next year? You've got to think about that.'

This remark was tantamount to poking a bear. 'Who cares about bloody Uni? I don't. Oh, and according to my parents it can't be just any Uni. It's got to be the best, with loads of posh rich kids. I'd rather stay here with you and work in a shop.'

He laughed. 'I can't see you behind a checkout at Tesco's Pheebs.'

Angered by his flippancy she shouted, 'There, you see! Nobody takes me seriously, including you.'

Dwain was tiring of this self-centred petulance. 'Listen Phoebe, your parents only want what's best for you and George. You're a clever girl with opportunities and a future many kids would die for.'

She sniffed contemptuously. 'Like who?'

He replied sharply, 'Well for a starter there's me and Zed.'

Surprised at this admission, she asked, 'What! You would have gone to Uni?'

He stood up shaking his head. 'Phoebe, you don't realise how bloody lucky you are. Living on a rough housing estate in South London we were never given the chance. For our parents it was often survival of the fittest.'

He was about to insist she rang her mother when a call came through on his mobile. It was George. 'Hey dude, I guess Phoebe is with you? I told mum not to worry, that's where she'll be. They're always at each other's throats lately.'

'She's a bit upset, that's all,' said Dwain as he handed the phone to Phoebe. 'Here, talk to George.'

Reluctantly she took it from him. 'Before you ask, I'm not coming home.'

George laughed. 'Well, that's alright then, you don't have to.'

Dropping her guard she asked, 'How do you mean?'

George, not always the most tolerant of his head strong sister said, 'I spoke to mum after you stormed out. She's prepared to meet you half way. You can stay with Dwain tonight, but you must come home tomorrow.' Then keeping his voice low, he whispered, 'But just be sensible sis.'

She laughed. 'What like you and Zed are?'

He replied. 'Yeah, but we can't get pregnant.'

It was another hour before Ron returned. He knocked gently on the door. 'Alright to come in?'

Dwain called out, 'Of course Ron, it's your boat.'

As usual Frankie and Freddie preceded him. Phoebe stiffened as they bolted through the door.

Ron grinned. 'So, all sorted, are we?'

Phoebe stood up from the sofa, put her arms around Ron's neck and planted a kiss on his cheek. 'Thanks for everything Ron. I must seem pretty silly.'

Blushing slightly, he said, 'Not at all my love. These things happen in life.'

As they left Dwain put his hand on Ron's arm. 'Thanks mate.'

Even though it was nearly ten, the warmth of the day still lingered in Dwain's boat. He pulled down the roller blinds and turned on a sidelight. 'I've got some lager in the fridge. Do you fancy one?'

Phoebe nodded. 'Cool.' Then kicking off her trainers she stretched full length on the sofa.

In the galley he found some crisps and opened the last two cans of Carling which were all that was left of the dozen Dwain, George and Zed had consumed a week ago. Neither Dwain nor Zed had asked where George had obtained them and providing it wasn't drugs they didn't much care. Though nearly eighteen, they were always careful to hide the evidence just in case Peggy came on one of her random boat inspections.

Lifting her legs up he sat down on the sofa next to her. She rested them back across his knees. After returning from school that afternoon, and before her altercation with her mother, she had changed into a pair of skinny faded blue jeans and a white 'Only One Earth' tee shirt. This was her latest thing. She and two other girls had nearly been suspended for trying to organise a sixth form 'School Strike for Climate Action'. Needless to say, her parents Lord and Lady Barrington Gore were not amused.

Looking into Dwain's eyes, she said, 'I've dreamt of this moment, just you and me alone on the boat.'

Teasing he asked. 'Oh yeah, and what else did you dream about?'

Giggling, she leant forward whispering in his ear.

'You know.'

They kissed, slow and sensually. She ran her hand inside his shirt and across his chest. He sighed deeply, 'I've got some in the drawer.'

Giggling innocently, she asked, 'Some what?'

Taking her by the hand he pulled her towards the bedroom. 'Come and find out.'

CHAPTER TWENTY FIVE

Interrogation

With every glass of whisky, and without any meaningful information about Roy Coombs' file forthcoming, Jimmy Doyle became more irritable with Peter Baxter. It had been over two hours since he had been forcibly taken from his betting shop in Sparkbrook to the Blue Diamond club. Now his nerves were starting to fray. With no windows in the small warm office, and the glare of the overhead lights, he could feel the sweat on his back and brow.

Jimmy's questioning was relentless and determined. One moment he would draw menacingly close. With clenched fists he would loudly accuse him of lying. Desperate efforts by Peter to deny this were met with another tirade of accusations. Then his anger would subside. Saying nothing, he would lean back in his chair, light a cigar and stare across the desk at him.

This silent intimidation unsettled Peter the most. It was as if Jimmy were weighing up the need for a more 'physical hands on approach' which no doubt his heavies would enjoy facilitating. It was during one of these lulls in interrogation that Jimmy, as if bored with this cat and mouse game suddenly told the two heavies to take Peter back to the shop.

Relieved, Peter asked, 'So, you believe me then?'

Jimmy stood up, his dark eyes boring into him. 'I'm giving you the benefit of the doubt.' He pointed, saying chillingly, 'But remember, I know where you live and the location of your shop. If you've been holding out on me, you'll regret it.'

As the heavy with the lion tattoo on his neck took Peter by the arm ushering him towards the door, Jimmy added, 'And it wouldn't be wise to mention to the old bill about our little conversation.'

They passed through the club where the lights were now on, enabling him to catch a glimpse of this dingy open space with its round tables, stage and bar. The smell of stale beer and cigarette smoke pervaded the air. Behind the bar a young man cleaning glasses watched as he was led out of the building.

Outside Peter drank in a mouthful of fresh air, curbing an overwhelming need to vomit. Overhead the trains rumbled in and out of Birmingham New Street Station. A line of wheelie bins, all overflowing stood on the opposite side of the service road and a large rat scuttled along the kerb. The back door of the car was opened, and he climbed in. The two heavies sat in the front. The one with the roaring lion tattoo drove.

Suddenly, instead of relief, Peter felt a bile of panic rise in his throat and wondered, 'Was this really a journey home or conveyance to something more sinister?'

Watching him in the mirror, the driver said, 'Don't worry mate, you'll live to see another day.'

The other laughed. 'For the moment anyway.'

For the remainder of the journey Peter stayed silent. Closing his eyes he tried to shut out the inane infantile prattle of the two heavies. Eventually, after navigating the early afternoon city traffic they turned onto Sparkbrook High Street. The passenger chuckled. 'Bit of a shit 'ole this place.'

Peter smiled at the irony considering where they had just come from.

Part way along, the driver suddenly hit the brakes and pulled into the kerb. Forced to swerve, a passing cyclist swore and gave him the finger as he rode by.

'You better get out here mate, looks like you have company,' said the driver.

Peter Baxter looked over his shoulder through the windscreen. Parked outside his betting shop was a police car. He opened the rear door and stepped out onto the pavement. The two heavies did a quick U turn and with a screech of tyres sped off in the opposite direction. Peter Baxter made a mental note of the type and registration number of the car. It might be useful later.

The shop door was open. Inside a few regular early punters were studying form in the racing papers. His manager and the police officer were talking by the counter. Peter greeted them.

His manager turned. 'Peter, where the hell have you been? When I arrived, the door was unlocked and no sign of you. I thought you'd been.........'

Peter stopped him. 'I'm so sorry. After unlocking this morning, I had to rush off to a meeting. I must have forgotten to lock up.'

The officer smiled. 'Well no harm done then. Just as well to be on the safe side.' He slipped his notebook back into his pocket. 'Thanks for the tea.'

After he had gone Peter asked his manager if he had said anything to the police about the Hicks and Ali's protection racket. He replied he hadn't then asked, 'So, what really happened to you?'

Exhausted by his recent experience, Peter replied, 'I need a strong coffee. Come into the office and I'll tell you all about it.'

On the short journey by cab from the Cottage to Tiddledurn High Street, Peggy felt a deep sense of foreboding for her friend. Betty had been feeling unwell for some time. Her breathing had become progressively worse, rendering her less mobile. Occasionally when Zed had mentioned it to her, she would bat it away saying, 'there's nothing for you to worry about son.'

But Peggy knew otherwise. Several weeks ago, when they were alone in Betty's flat she had confided in Peggy about her heart problems. At the same time, she had passed Peggy a large brown envelope, saying, 'This contains everything you would need in case anything happens to me. There is also a letter to Zed.'

Peggy, who had earlier agreed to be her executor, took it from her joking, 'You'll probably out live all of us.'

Betty had laughed at this suggestion saying, 'I'm not sure I want to.'

Standing outside Strout's butcher's shop, Peggy and Zed immediately noticed that Betty's first floor flat was in darkness.

Zed was worried 'That's odd. She never goes to bed before midnight.'

Trying to reassure him Peggy replied, 'Well, if she felt unwell, she may have done so.' Although both knew this was unlikely.

Using her spare key Peggy opened the front door and switched on the light at the bottom of the stairs. Zed called out, 'Gran, it's me and Peggy.'

There was no answer. At the top of the stairs were four wood panelled doors leading off a narrow hallway. The nearest was the sitting room. Peggy opened it and turned on the light. Betty was sitting in her armchair, her head tilting to one side.

The curtains were still open as was one window. The television was off. This was no surprise as, apart from the soaps, she often described the programmes as rubbish. At first, they thought she was asleep. Zed touched her arm.

'Wakey, wakey Gran.'

Seeing Betty's greying pallor, Peggy instantly realised what had happened. She gently lifted her limp wrist to feel for a pulse.

There was none.

Anxiously Zed asked, 'What's the matter with her. Why won't she wake up?' Again, he tugged her arm, 'Gran, Gran, come on it's me, Zed.'

Looking at him Peggy momentarily remembered the eleven year old boy who had recently lost his mum to drugs. Now his beloved gran, who had always been there for him had gone as well.

She put her arm around his shoulder and pulled him close to her, saying softly, 'Zed, my love, your gran has died. I'm so sorry.'

At first, he said nothing, trying to take in the enormity of what had occurred.

He stared down at the familiar grey haired figure sitting motionless in the chair. Her reading glasses hung from a silver cord which rested on her chest. The red woollen cardigan patterned with small butterflies was unbuttoned. Peggy had bought it for her last Christmas after she complained about feeling cold in the evenings. On her lap, a paperback by her favourite author, Nora Roberts, lay open. Two fingers rested on a page as if about to turn it over. The gold wedding ring she refused to take off contrasted with the paleness of her slender fingers. On a small side table alongside a framed picture of Zed and his mum was a cold cup of tea and two biscuits.

It was ten o'clock. In the cottage Tim had just made a brew and a sandwich. He wouldn't go to bed until Peggy and Zed returned. Dwain was in his boat with Phoebe, their thoughts on one thing only. Fortunately, he had left his phone on. Rocket Ron who never slept well had nodded off in his chair. His two ferrets, Frankie and Freddie, asleep by his feet. Albert Strout the butcher had just returned home from a Chamber of Commerce meeting in Melbury. George was at the Manor House with his parents. He was in bed, though looking at gay porn on his laptop.

Soon the often disregarded 'cycle of life' would impact upon them, and for each in their own way their landscape would be changed forever.

Peggy had gone into the bedroom, taken a sheet from the bed and covered Betty with it. Now her priority was Zed. He was sitting on the sofa. His tear stained face a frozen mask of sorrow. She made the call to Tim. It was five minutes past ten.

CHAPTER TWENTY SIX

Loose Tongues

After two weeks of waiting, Beaky Quin had received a text from the Romanian lad. They agreed to meet outside the club after his shift had finished at midnight. Beaky wouldn't want to risk Jimmy Doyle seeing them talking together. He sat waiting in the 'Solomon Cutter' pub in Gas Street basin. Outside the bright street lights reflected off the still waters of the murky canal.

It was one of the few bars open until one o'clock and only a ten minute walk from the Blue Diamond Club. Most of the clientele were young and lively, leaving him feeling distinctly out of place. He spotted the Romanian lad pushing his way through the throng.

As the lad sat down opposite him, Beaky noticed a cut and bruise under his left eye. 'What happened there?'

The lad put his hand to his swollen cheek. 'It was last night. Some drunken man said he didn't want to be served by a fucking immigrant. When I asked him to stop swearing, he hit me, telling me to piss off home.'

Beaky shook his head. 'Damn scumbag.'

The lad continued. 'Anyway, Jimmy's two heavies saw him do it and threw him out. When they came back inside they offered to buy me a drink. One even gave me a wet tea towel to hold over my eye.'

Beaky laughed. 'They're all heart those two.' He took a sip of his lager.

'So, what have you got for me?' Unbeknown to the Romanian lad, Beaky was recording the conversation on his phone. He was taking no chances in case the lad later denied saying it. Anxiously looking around him the lad moved his chair closer to Beaky.

'For the rest of the night both the heavies sat at the bar drinking beer and whisky. One asked which

177

country I had come from. I told him Romania. The other with the tattoo asked me if that was in Italy.'

Beaky sighed. 'No surprises there then, thick as two planks.'

The lad continued. 'Anyway, the other one said, I'd be alright 'ere. As long as I behaved myself Jimmy would look after me. So, I asked them what they did for Jimmy?'

'That was brave of you.'

'They were well drunk by then. Both laughed at my question. The one with the earing told me they did anything and everything as Jimmy doesn't like getting his hands dirty. He leaves the rough stuff to them.'

Beaky was getting impatient but didn't interrupt him.

'So, I asked them, like what? By now their words were getting slurred and I was having difficulty understanding them. Suddenly the one with the tattoo leant across the bar and grabbed my shoulder. Then making a shape of a gun with his hand pointed at me saying, bang, bang, boom, boom. Then sat back laughing.'

Beaky was shocked. 'Wow! That's some admission. They must have been pretty drunk. So, what did you say?'

'Well, I knew what bang, bang, meant, but not boom, boom. So again, I asked them. The other one said, 'You know son, a little bit of Semtex, and…' Then standing up from the stool he threw his arms in the air, shouting Boom. Boom.'

'Did anyone else hear them?' asked Beaky.

The lad shrugged. 'I doubt it, the music was very loud.'

Beaky was quiet for a moment as he considered the significance of this information. 'Well done son, you've done good, my friends will be pleased.'

'So, this will help me to stay in England?'

Beaky stood up. 'No problem son. Don't worry about it, now I must be going.'

The following morning Beaky Quin sat opposite DCI Collins and his DS, with a plain wooden table between them. Earlier he had been lifted by the DS and taken to the National Crime Agency's obscure office on a nearby trading estate. After his previous late night at the Blue Diamond Club he was feeling tired and fragile. The last thing he needed was an interrogation by the police Commenting on his dishevelled appearance the DCI apologised for the early call.

Unimpressed by this gibing Beaky replied, 'I was out doing your bidding, if you must know.'

The DCI smiled. 'Good, that's why you're here.'

Beaky breathed in heavily hoping a sudden intake of oxygen would keep him awake. 'Is there any chance of a coffee?'

Studying his bloodshot eyes the DCI chortled. 'Of course. Anything to stimulate those little grey cells of yours.'

The DS stood up, saying sarcastically, 'Would sir like toast and jam?'

Beaky ignored him.

While they were waiting the DCI asked, 'I still don't understand why you got involved in that break in at the marina. It wasn't your bag.'

Realising there was no further point in prevaricating Beaky said, 'You don't say no to Jimmy Doyle if you value your health.'

The DCI grinned. 'And you were looking for the Roy Coombs' file on Hicks and Ali, is that right?'

Surprised by the question Beaky asked, 'How did you…...?'

'Elementary, my dear Watson, elementary.'

Beaky looked confused. 'Who's Watson?'

Once back in the room the DS placed a cup of coffee in front of Beaky.

DCI Collins continued, 'Right my friend, things have moved on. We need to know what you have for us.'

The DS added sharply, 'And it better be good.'

Unlike his senior officer he did little to hide his contempt for people like Beaky. Whilst the need for snouts was important in crime detection, it often meant their own criminal activities were overlooked.

Feeling slightly more attentive Beaky said, 'I think I have a juicy bone for you to gnaw on.'

The DCI sucked the end of his pen. 'Let's hope for your sake it's got plenty of meat on it.'

Beaky took another sip of the hot coffee then took his phone from his pocket. Placing it on the table he switched on the recording of the Romanian lad. Occasionally the DCI would interrupt him to ask a question or seek clarification. Both detectives were concerned about the inebriated state of the two heavies and whether that would compromise their story.

The DS put it to him bluntly. 'You don't think they were bullshitting him?'

Beaky suggested that knowing their reputation for violence he doubted it. When he had finished Beaky sat back and took another mouthful of the now cooling coffee. For a moment both detectives remained silent.

Then the DCI asked, 'Do these two individuals have names?'

Beaky trawled his mind. 'I think the one with the neck tattoo is called Terry. The other one is known as Dibs.'

'Why Dibs?'

Beaky shrugged. 'Who knows?'

The DCI's mobile rang. After glancing at the screen, he stood up and went to leave the room. Turning to Beaky, he said, 'Don't go anywhere.'

Crestfallen, Beaky managed a weak smile. The call was from his office saying that a Peter Baxter was trying to get hold of him urgently. He made a note of the number then put the phone back in his pocket. Leaving Beaky on his own he called the DS outside.

'We need to pick up the two laughing boys.'

'We don't have an address for them Guv.'

The DCI shrugged. 'Lift them from the club later. It might provoke a response from Jimmy Doyle.'

'Shall we bring them here?'

Smiling mischievously, the DCI answered, 'No, take them to the nick. I want them to be seen.' As the DS turned to go Collins added, 'Go mob handed, they sound a bit tasty.'

Beaky's eyes focused on the four bare walls which surrounded him. With every breath his chest felt heavier as if he was slowly suffocating. Suppressing a groan of despair, he bit down hard on his upper forefinger. He knew any future he had was caught in a vice between DCI Collins and Jimmy Doyle. Whatever the police officer decided it was the retribution of Jimmy Doyle he feared the most.

Beaky Quin's trepidation was palpable as DCI Collins entered the room. Sitting down, he felt a flicker of sympathy for this sad and dejected little man.

'Right Mr Quin, we've decided your information is genuine and we'll act on it. Later today these two men will be arrested and taken to the police station for questioning.'

Beaky was worried. 'But what about the lad? They'll know where the information came from?'

'He'll be arrested and handed to the immigration people. After all, you said he was an illegal.'

Beaky looked sullen at this unexpected outcome, but the DCI had his measure. 'Feeling guilty, are we? And so you should. You used this lad for your own ends, irrespective of the consequences.'

Beaky said nothing to the officer about the promise he had made to him.

Collins stood up. 'Right, we're done here. 'You're free to go.'

'You won't be revealing my involvement to anyone?'

The DCI looked him in the eye. 'No, but I suggest a permanent change of scenery might be good.'

CHAPTER TWENTY SEVEN

Zed's Despair

It had been a week since Betty's death and there was little joy inside the cottage by the lock. Zed had retreated inside himself to a place where even Dwain could not reach him. Although of course he had been upset when his mum had died, this was different, very different. To him Betty had been his rock, his only biological link to his past life in South London. Since his birth she had been a surrogate mother, always there as a safety net when her drug prone daughter had struggled and failed with the responsibilities of motherhood. Because of this he had never thought of himself as an orphan. Now he was.

Although upset by the sudden loss of Betty, ever the pragmatist, Tim had returned to work at the marina. He still suffered from the side effects of the violent attack on him by Beaky Quin, though chose to keep the occasional dizzy spells and tiredness to himself. He knew that despite the sterling efforts of his two apprentices Zed and Dwain, there would be a backlog of engineering work to be completed. With Zed now temporarily out of action he would have to rely on just Dwain to help.

He and Peggy had argued about this. She felt Zed needed time on his own to grieve. Tim though, thought being occupied with work was the best and quickest way for him to deal with it. As was often the way with these discussions, Peggy prevailed.

They were in a sombre mood that morning when they drove into the marina. In contrast a vast expanse of cloudless blue sky embraced the verdant landscape. Shafts of golden sunlight glistened on the rippling waters. Small groups of mallards and swans floated contentedly from boat to boat seeking breakfast. The early morning air smelt fresh and scented like a newly mown lawn. Whilst Tim and Dwain headed for the workshop, Peggy unlocked the office and went inside. She had offered to stay at home with Zed, but he preferred to be alone.

After making a cup of tea she sat at her desk and turned on the computer. In an instant the screen was flooded with recent emails. She sighed and turned it off. The answer phone was equally filled. Slowly sipping the herbal brew she glanced around the small office. Suddenly she was gripped by an overwhelming sense of despondency. Peggy had always been a 'glass half full' person but recent events had gradually eroded her and Tim's resilience. In the years since Betty had been living in Tiddledurn they had become close, sharing laughs and secrets as only two mature women could. Now her good friend was gone. A tear ran down her cheek as she remembered her.

She stood up and crossed the room to the window overlooking the marina. It looked so calm and tranquil as moored boats bobbed gently against their pontoons. But Peggy was only too aware of the hard work and time needed to maintain this idyll and the business it supported. For some time now she had been considering the future. She and Tim were getting no younger and though he wouldn't admit it she knew he was struggling. She often wished Zed and Dwain were older and more experienced, but they were not yet eighteen.

Taking out her mobile phone she rang Zed. There was no answer. Again, she called. Still no reply. Closing and locking the office door she walked across to the workshop. Tim, always enthusiastically up to his elbow in engine parts, was busying himself re-organising a shelf; his mind clearly somewhere else.

Standing in front of a vice Dwain was half heartily sawing through a metal pipe.

'I can't get through to Zed,' said Peggy. 'I'm going to call a cab and go home.'

Tim needed no prompting, 'Don't worry about a cab. We'll come to.'

When the land rover pulled up outside the cottage Zed was sitting on the balance beam staring down into the empty lock chamber. A gentle trickle of water fell from the leaky gates above. On the opposite side of the canal a combine harvester threw dust high into the air as it threshed the summer crop. He was deep in thought as he read through the letter his gran had written to him before she died.

Dwain walked over and sat next to him. 'Hi dude, how you doing?'

For a moment Zed didn't answer then he smiled. 'I'm glad Gran ended her days down here rather than in South London. She loved this place.'

Dwain put his arm around Zed's shoulder. 'Yeah, me too.'

Watching this affectionate interaction from the window Peggy breathed a sigh of relief. She had seen the smile on Zed's face and knew in time all would be well. Opening the window she called, 'You two up for lunch?' They both waved.

Neither Tim nor Peggy returned to the marina that day. In the afternoon Zed and Dwain walked to the village to meet Phoebe and George from school.

Lady Barrington Gore was as usual waiting for them in her Range Rover. She had invited Zed and Dwain to the Manor House for tea. Although still unaware of the relationship between Zed and George, she had finally come to accept her daughter's teenage romance with Dwain. It wasn't that she didn't like Dwain it was just in bred snobbery, as Phoebe often reminded her. Lady Barrington Gore would always defend it as 'wanting the best' for her daughter.

The unmarked police car and a van pulled up outside the Blue Diamond Club. It was early evening and they had calculated that it would not be busy. With the detective sergeant were five plain clothes and two uniformed officers. All were wearing stab vests, carrying nightsticks and handcuffs. Given the reputation of the two men they had come for, they were taking no chances.

The bouncer guarding the door eyeballed them as they alighted from the vehicles. The sergeant weighed him up: well built, close cropped hair with a boxer's nose and thick muscles protruding from his tight black tee shirt. After seeing his warrant card, the bouncer reluctantly stood aside and let them pass.

The interior of the club was dimly lit and the air stale and heavy. Oblivious to the incomers a few of the regulars sat drinking at the round tables. The two heavies, obvious from the description the sergeant had been given were as usual propping up the bar. The sergeant gave a signal and the pre rehearsed arrest plan begun. Quickly and quietly the officers moved forward surrounding the two men, both now pretty inebriated. The two uniformed officers stood some feet away, their Tasers pointed towards the group. Should the two heavies attempt to break free they would feel the full force of the 1500 volt sting.

This was the moment of danger. Would they resist or come quietly. For the heavies the latter would not be an option. Again, the sergeant showed his warrant card saying, 'Police, we need you to come with us.'

The one sporting the neck tattoo turned and laughed. 'What the fuck for?'

Remaining calm, the sergeant replied, 'You are being arrested on suspicion of murder and arson.'

Without warning the heavy swung a punch catching the sergeant on the nose. The low thudding noise was followed by a spurt of bright red blood. As the sergeant reeled backwards three of the detectives pulled their night sticks hitting the assailant hard on the arm and shoulder. Yanking him from the stool they forced him to the floor. Whilst two knelt on his back the other pulled his hands together and applied the handcuffs. Though still screaming expletives he was no longer a risk to them.

The second heavy had grabbed an empty glass from the bar to use as a weapon. Another detective delivered a swift punch to his solar plexus which soon disarmed him. He too was quickly pushed onto the floor and cuffed. It was only at this point that the uniformed officers returned their Tasers to their holsters. Fearing it was a raid, a few of the regulars had swiftly slipped away. Others watched in disbelief as the struggling heavies were lifted to their feet. Wiping blood from his nose the sergeant cautioned them, adding assaulting a police officer and resisting arrest to the charge sheet.

Whilst they were being dragged outside to the waiting police van the sergeant turned his attention to the young Romanian lad who had been serving behind the bar. During the fracas he had fled from the bar to a nearby table. Now he was petrified that the two heavies would suspect him of talking. He had though convinced himself that spying for Beaky Quin had been the right thing to do in the circumstances. His reward would be asylum in the UK. He was about to move back behind the bar when the sergeant and one of the uniformed officers approached him.

'Young man, I'm arresting you on suspicion of being in the country illegally.'
The uniformed officer told him to put his hands behind his back. As the handcuffs were being applied, the lad desperately pleaded with them. 'No, no, please you

don't understand. Mr Quin say if I help police I can stay in country.'

The officer laughed. 'Yeah, sure mate, tell that to the immigration people.'

As he was led away still protesting the sergeant said, 'Put him in the car not in the van with those two scum bags.' Before leaving, the sergeant cast an eye around the murky cavern. He had been hoping Jimmy Doyle would be there. Still, no matter the word of their arrest would soon get back to him.

CHAPTER TWENTY EIGHT

Peggy's Promise

Alone in the cottage with Tim, Peggy decided to broach the subject which had been troubling her for some time. He had settled into his chair and was reading a letter which was on the mat when they had returned from the marina. She sat down opposite him. Shaking his head in despair, he said, 'You'll never believe this Peg. It's from Melbury Police. They're not going to do anything more about the break in.'

Peggy took the letter from him and read it.

With regard to the burglary and assault at your premises. After a thorough investigation and subsequent arrest of a suspect, we have now been advised by the CPS that there is insufficient evidence to secure a prosecution and therefore will not be proceeding any further with the case.

In disbelief she asked, 'What about this Quin character? I thought they had fingerprints from the hire boat he stayed on?'

Tim nodded. 'Yeah and they also found a bag which belonged to him, what about that as evidence? Christ they could have killed me.' He shrugged apathetically. 'It all smells a bit fishy to me. It doesn't give you much faith in the bloody law.'

Although sharing his annoyance, the timing of this letter and Tim's frustration and anger could not have been better for Peggy. This presented her with the opportunity to discuss the marina.

'Tim, we need to talk about the marina.'

He nodded. 'I'm listening.'

This itself was a step forward. But what happened next was even more of a surprise to her.

'I know what you're thinking Peg and I agree with you. It's time to call it a day. I've been considering it too. It was a good idea when we took it on, but things have changed. My only worry though is for the boys. They're nearing the end of their apprenticeship at Melbury College and they're going to need work and a future.'

Peggy smiled. She had already considered this dilemma and had a plan to put to him. The concern wasn't just for the boys. She knew that without something to do Tim would be like a bear with a sore head, and she couldn't deal with that.

'I'll make a brew. There's something else we need to discuss.'

He laughed. 'Blimey you have been doing a lot of thinking lately.'

Whilst in the kitchen she rehearsed her forthcoming conversation with Tim. She had been mulling this over for some time. Although this was something she had promised Betty, her hope was that the day would not come. But it had and it was now time to activate that promise to her friend.

Tim's facial expressions were always difficult to read. He rarely did emotion or annoyance. It did though take little to nudge him towards irritability, particularly with fools and petty officials. After making two mugs of tea Peggy sat back down with Tim and outlined the promise and commitment she had made to Betty before her death. He listened carefully, occasionally stroking his now greying beard. At one point Peggy had to stop and regain her composure, such was her distress at the loss of her good friend. It was so sudden, so sad.

When she had finished, nervously she asked him. 'Well, what do you think?'

Without answering he stood up, crossed the room and opened the sideboard door. Taking out a bottle of whisky he said, 'I think I need something stronger than tea.'

She watched as he poured himself a large glass before returning to his chair. Thinking for a moment, he asked, 'Don't we have to be.......' He paused. '......er married or something?'

Peggy laughed. 'I thought you'd never ask.' The mere mention of conjugality prompted Tim to take an even larger swig of whisky.

Peggy continued. 'I looked it up. The law changed in 2012. The only requirement now is that the couple must be in a stable, enduring, family relationship and the child be under eighteen years.'

Tim asked innocently, 'Is that us then?'

She nodded. 'Well, after all this time I would say so, wouldn't you?'

He took another drink of whisky, this time slowly swirling the velvety liquid around his mouth. Peggy waited until the Laphroaig single malt oiled his cognitive wheels.

Suddenly he laughed. 'Well, if that's what Betty wanted then why not?'

Surprised by the sudden decision Peggy asked, 'So, you agree then?'

Tim smiled. 'Of course I do. I love that boy as if he were my own. Always have done.'

A tear ran down Peggy's cheek at this rare sentimental admission. 'I know you do, as do I.'

'But, what about Zed? Maybe he doesn't want to be adopted by us.'

She walked over giving him a kiss on the cheek. 'I think you underestimate him, he regards you as a father now. This just makes it legal. My only concern is Dwain, will he feel left out; after all they're like brothers.'

Tim shrugged. 'He'll understand. He's a strong character, and anyway, unlike Zed, he still has a family in London. Not that he ever sees them.'

'We'll speak to Zed tonight.'

Tim chuckled. 'That's if they're back before midnight.'

After a night in the stark police cells the bravado of the two heavies had significantly subsided. Whether it was the process of sobering up or the realisation of their dilemma was unclear. No doubt a bit of both. After the custody officer had unlocked the cell doors both men walked meekly along the passage to their interview with DCI Collins and the woman officer from the National Crime Agency. Their nervousness at what awaited them was palpable.

In his office DCI Collins checked his watch, it was nine thirty. A cool breeze blew in from an open window as he and his colleague from the NCA devised their questioning strategy. Over mugs of strong coffee, they both agreed that so far, their evidence against the two men was flimsy to say the least.

The detectives' only leverage was firstly, a recorded conversation at the Blue Diamond Club with the Romanian lad and secondly, a traffic enforcement camera image showing their car on the M4 motorway. It had been taken on the same day as the explosion and only miles from the marina. They knew that neither of these would stand up to scrutiny in court.

So they decided to go in hard, embellishing the facts slightly, to appear that they had more substantial evidence. These two men might be hard on the outside, but the detectives knew they would crumble under intense interrogation. The two dim-witted goons were only feed for the sharks. It was the person who had recruited them and constructed the bomb that they wanted to arrest; their prime suspect being Jimmy Doyle, the boss of the Blue Diamond Club.

The DCI smiled as he recounted the phone call he had received at home last night from Detective Superintendent Turner. It had been loud and aggressive demanding to know why two of Jimmy Doyle's men had been arrested. The DCI had smiled to himself. Clearly the club owner had contacted his 'patsy' for answers. The DCI had explained calmly the reasons for the arrest, although it was obvious from the DSU's agitated response that his screws were being turned hard. He thought he caught a flicker of mirth on his female colleague's face, after all no one liked a bent copper. But no. She was indeed a cold fish.

Before leaving his office, Collins called Peter Baxter. He wanted Amit Thakur to attend an identity parade, suspecting that it was the two heavies who had assaulted his nephew at the Indian restaurant. As he had not spoken to the DCI for some time Peter asked if anymore had been discovered about the Roy Coombs file of evidence on Hicks and Ali. The DCI batted the question away, again saying that it was still a part of a larger ongoing police operation.

What he didn't disclose was that from early on, the file had been in the hands of the NCA. They had painstakingly followed up every strand of documented evidence and along with investigations by the drugs and vice squads were now ready to arrest and charge Duncan Hicks and Sahil Ali, on their release from prison.

CHAPTER TWENTY NINE

I Love You

Much to everyone's relief, afternoon tea at the Manor House had finished at six. Whilst Lady Barrington Gore had tried to make it as informal as possible, Zed and Dwain felt stressed at having to be on their best behaviour. Afterwards Phoebe and George had a couple of hours to spend time with their friends in their respective bedrooms. Although her mother still had concerns about boyfriends in her daughter's bedroom, to keep the peace she reluctantly said nothing. She never though gave a thought to what 'activities' George and Zed ever got up to in his bedroom. This ongoing deception always amused her son.

Zed and George lay together on his bed sharing an earpiece as they listened to music on George's smartphone. His room was the opposite of Phoebe's; clothes strewn across the floor, discarded cola cans and a rubbish bin overflowing with screwed up paper. His mother had long ago given up on nagging him to tidy it.

'How are you feeling about your gran now?' asked George.

'Alright I suppose, though I really miss her,' replied Zed, as his fingers strummed to the music.

'When is the funeral?'

Zed shook his head. 'There's not going to be one.'

Surprised, George pulled the earpiece out. 'How do you mean dude? No funeral? All dead people have a funeral.'

'Peggy said Gran wanted one of those quickie things.'

George laughed. 'What the hell's a quickie funeral?'

Zed shrugged. 'I dunno really. Apparently, they just cremate you, without anyone being there. Then send you the ashes afterwards.'

George grimaced. 'That sounds creepy to me man.'

Zed rested his head on George's shoulder. 'I suppose I'm officially an orphan now.'

George kissed him on the forehead. 'It doesn't matter dude. You're still the same person and I love you.'

Zed was quiet for a moment then asked, 'And what happens when you go to Uni next year? I'll lose you too.'

George rolled over on top of Zed, pinning him down. 'No, you bloody won't, so get that out of your head now.'

A similar conversation had often taken place between Phoebe and Dwain, and despite her sincere pledges he was, like Tim, a pragmatist. She was an intelligent good looking girl from an upper middle class family. He was a working class boy from a rough South London Housing estate. He knew that during her forthcoming years at a distant university she would meet good looking, clever boys from the same background as her: no doubt all the better, in Lady Barrington's Gore's eyes, if they happened to come from a wealthy family.

It was just after nine when Lady Barrington Gore dropped Zed and Dwain back to the cottage. Even though Zed and Dwain now lived on the boats they always called in to the cottage if the lights were on. When they opened the door Tim was asleep in his chair and Peggy was reading.

'Oh, sorry are we disturbing you?' asked Zed.

Peggy looked up. 'Not at all love, we wanted to talk with you. Wake up Tim, the boys are here.'

He groaned, insisting he wasn't asleep just resting his eyes. Zed and Dwain sat down on the sofa.

Dwain joked. 'So, what have we done wrong now?'

Tim replied humorously, 'For once, nothing.'

'It's nothing like that, love. There's something important we need to ask you.'

Zed sensed a mood change. 'That sounds serious.'

Peggy smiled. 'Well, in a way it is love.' Suddenly she hesitated not quite sure how to phrase the question.

Impatiently Tim interrupted, 'For god's sake woman just ask him.'

Zed was confused. 'Ask me what?'

Before Peggy could speak, Tim said bluntly, 'Now that your gran's gone would you like us to adopt you?' He paused. 'Officially.'

Zed was stunned. He looked at Dwain, then to Peggy and back to Tim.

'What, you mean become my parents?'

'Yes, that's what it would mean love. It was what your gran wanted if anything happened to her before you were eighteen.'

Dwain nudged him. 'Well go on say something dude.' He laughed. 'You can adopt me as well if you like.'

Horrified, for a moment Peggy thought Zed might say no. Then with a beaming smile he replied, 'Yeah, that'll be cool.'

Peggy stood up. 'Oh, I'm so pleased love. Give me a hug.'

Watching this tactile embrace Tim shook his head, 'Daft buggers.'

Peggy breathed a sigh of relief. 'Right tomorrow I'll get the ball rolling.'

Before the boys left the cottage that evening Peggy said, 'There is something else we need to discuss with you, but we'll leave that for tomorrow.'

Dwain laughed. 'Blimey you're not getting married are you?'

Peggy winked. 'See you tomorrow boys.'

After news of the arrests Jimmy Doyle was steaming. Those two boneheads in police custody didn't have a brain between them. God knows what they might be saying. He had earlier called one of his dodgy solicitor friends to attend the station and act on their behalf. Now he was waiting anxiously for him to report back. He had decided against contacting Hicks and Ali in prison. Unlike the victims of their protection racket, they were looking forward to their imminent release.

In any case there was nothing for them to be concerned about. There was no direct evidence linking them to the explosion at the marina and the subsequent death of Roy Coombs. Jimmy Doyle shuddered and swore to himself. 'Why the hell did I go along with it?'

Due to the incriminating evidence in his journalist file Hicks and Ali had been desperate to close Roy Coombs down. Knowing as they did of Jimmy's past history in Northern Ireland, he would be the ideal man for the job. Although being their friend and business associate Jimmy had always tried to distance himself from Hicks and Ali's more extreme and risky activities. This had not always been possible and now this act of stupidity could lead back to his door. But first he needed to understand what, or who had led the police to his two heavies and the Romanian lad.

He went into the bar poured himself a large brandy and returned to his office. After lighting a cigar, he closed his eyes forcing himself to remain calm whilst he mulled over recent events. There had to be a link, he was missing something. Occasionally his thoughts were disturbed as a nearby train rattled into New Street Station. There was only one name which came to mind, Beaky Quin. He had been at the club a lot lately and had been seen talking to the Romanian lad. But what reason would he have to grass, other than being pissed off he didn't get paid for the bungled marina burglary.

Whilst waiting for the call from the solicitor he considered three possible outcomes from the police questioning of the heavies. They would either stay quiet, in which case the police would have to prove their guilt. Or under pressure, they would admit their involvement but not implicate him.

It was the third which worried him the most and regrettably was the most likely. The police, knowing that the two heavies were only small fry would offer them deals and inducements to squeal like pigs. This would bring the old bill knocking on his door. This was a risk he couldn't take. Now he needed a plan, and fast.

It was raining. A low dark cloud hung over the open expanse of water. An ever increasing breeze jostled the moored boats, nudging them against the pontoons. It was the following day. Tim and Peggy sat with the boys in the marina office. Bewildered Zed asked, 'How do you mean give up the marina?'
Tim and Peggy had anticipated that this would be a difficult discussion, particularly so close after Betty's passing.
Dwain was also puzzled and asked, 'Why?'
Peggy sighed. 'Because neither of us is getting any younger, and it's becoming too much for us.'
Zed and Dwain found this hard to understand as they had always thought them so strong.
Tim added, 'Also, ever since that cretin hit me on the head, I keep getting these dizzy spells. The quack says they should go in time, but there's no guarantee.'
Peggy was surprised at this candid admission for he rarely spoke about his health or admitted to feeling unwell. She added. 'We were hoping to keep the business going long enough for you two to take over, but I'm afraid events have overtaken us.'
Helpfully Zed said, 'We could do it now.'
Tim laughed. 'Good thought lad, but that's not possible I'm afraid.'
'Well, what will you do then?' asked Dwain.
Tim chuckled. 'Good point son.' He knew Dwain really meant, 'What will we do?'
Recognising their concern Peggy said, 'There is an alternative plan which I put to Tim last night.'

Tim nodded, 'It sounds sensible lads, worth a try.'

'Why don't you get two cans of cola and we'll explain it to you?' said Peggy.

CHAPTER THIRTY

Time To Leave

One thing that Jimmy Doyle had learned during the troubles in Northern Ireland was how to stay one step in front of the authorities. This IRA tactic was well practiced, moving rapidly from one location to another, often with no more than they could carry. It was all about balancing risk to avoid being compromised: the destruction of potential evidence in their wake being key.

Sitting at his desk he had decided not to wait for the solicitor's phone call from the police station. The gamble was too great for him to take. He took one last look at the interior of the club, the successful business he had built up over the years. He would miss it, but his self-preservation had to come first.

He stubbed out his cigar and went into an outer room. Against a wall was a double stack of metal beer barrels. After lifting them to one side he placed a key in the lock of a concealed reinforced door. This led to a cellar where the tools of his deadly trade were kept. After switching on the light he descended the wooden stairs to the small underground space.

There were three heavy, steel cabinets. Two contained all the components required to construct different types of explosive devices; his speciality being time delayed explosions. Since moving to Birmingham his work had been in much demand from criminals across the country. Most were requests to carry out small to medium size jobs, safecracking, door blowing, or what were called' frightener' devices such as letter bombs. The bomb in Harry Martin's marina had been the largest he had constructed since leaving Northern Ireland. The third cabinet contained an assortment of weapons, mainly purchased by the underworld for their nefarious activities.

He picked up a stool and sat at the sturdy work bench, then switched on a powerful side lamp. Good vision was essential for this intricate work. One mistake could prove fatal. He knew it was too late to remove his arsenal or the compromising content on his office computer. If discovered by the police, it would seal his fate. Having once served five years in the Maze prison near Belfast, he had no intention of being banged up again.

Now he would make an even bigger timed device which would consign the club and everything in it to an inferno. He had paid off the bouncer and closed the club. By the time of the explosion, he would be gone. Two hours before detonation he would drive to Wolverhampton Halfpenny Green Airport where, courtesy of his Irish contacts, he would fly out of the country and the reach of the British Police.

In the marina office Tim and Peggy had just resumed their meeting with Dwain and Zed when a car pulled up outside. Surprised, Zed said, 'That's Harry's car.'
Peggy nodded. 'It is indeed, he's part of our long term plan.'
Harry Martin owned the marina, but following a heart attack some time ago had leased it to Tim. Zed and Dwain were pleased to see him. He had been good to them in the early days, giving them a job and helping them out financially.

Harry beamed when he saw them. 'My, my, how you two have grown. I say, how you have grown.' Harry always repeated himself.

'We're nearly eighteen now,' said Zed.
Harry laughed. 'Eighteen. And the world at your feet. I say world at your feet.' He pulled up a chair and

touched Zed on the shoulder. 'Sorry to hear about your gran lad. Sorry to hear.'

Peggy turned to Zed and Dwain and said, 'Well, as we told you we are going to give up running the marina. We've spoken to Harry and he's agreed to terminate the lease.'

Harry nodded. 'That's right. I say that's right.'

'So, who will run the marina then?' asked Dwain.

Harry smiled. 'Someone you once met. I say once met.'

The boys looked at each other trying to think who this person was.

Tim grinned. 'I seem to remember you were both besotted by her.'

As the penny slowly dropped, Zed asked, 'What, your niece Kate?'

Harry nodded, 'Quite so, I say quite so.'

Dwain added, 'Wow, she's fit man.'

Tim laughed, 'and way out of your league lad.' Then he asked, 'So, I expect you're wondering where this move leaves us?'

Eager to know both boys nodded.

Peggy continued, 'Well this is the plan. Kate will manage the day to day business of the marina, boat hire, moorings etc. But the maintenance of the hire boats and outside engineering work will stay with Tim and you two.'

'And we're going to set up a separate marine engineering company, which will give you lads long term job protection,' added Tim.

'So, we will still have jobs then?'

Peggy nodded. 'Of course love and just as important Tim will have something to keep him occupied.'

'Which I hope will become less once you two are qualified and take on more of the work,' said Tim.

The boys grinned at each other.

'That sounds really great, thanks.'

'Right then you two, I think that deserves a brew, then you can get back to work. There's plenty to do in the workshop.'

'See that Harry. He's a slave driver,' joked Zed. Harry laughed. 'It's a hard life, boys. I say a hard life.'

After they had left Tim told Harry about the letter he had received from Melbury Police.

'It's unbelievable,' said Peggy.

Without comment Harry suddenly stood up, crossed to the window and looked out over the marina.

'Are you alright Harry?' she asked.

For a moment he said nothing then turned.

'I have something to tell you. I say, something to tell you.'

Sitting back down, he took an envelope from his pocket. Withdrawing the letter inside it he handed it to Peggy. She scanned the header. It was from the National Crime Agency.

'What is it?' asked Tim.

She glanced at Harry then started to read aloud.

Dear Mr Martin,

With regard to Operation Ghost, we are at an end stage in our investigations where it would now be appropriate for you to share our past confidential discussions with your leaseholders at the marina. As explained at the time, as the people on the ground it was important for their own safety that they were unaware of this highly covert operation. It was also essential that the marina be seen to be operating as normal prior to this assassination attempt. Please apologise to them for any disruption or upset this may have caused.

Thank you for your co-operation and assisting us in bringing these people to justice.

Peggy looked up. 'I don't understand Harry. What confidential discussions?'

Sheepishly Harry said, 'The journalist, Roy Coombs, was staying here under police protection, but somebody leaked his location and the people who were after him arranged to have him killed, I say killed.'

Tim laughed sarcastically. 'Well so much for police protection, they got to him anyway.'

Harry hesitated then said, 'Well that's the point. They didn't. Let me explain, I say let me explain.'

The woman detective from the NCA allowed herself a brief smile of satisfaction as she and DCI Collins walked back from the interview room to his office. He noticed this brief glimmer of normality and chuckled to himself. She was human after all. It had taken four exhaustive hours, but their perseverance had paid off. Neither of the two heavies had the intellectual ability to withstand that level of questioning for long.

Even Jimmy Doyle's dodgy solicitor was flagging. Someone a bit more committed to his client's interests might have contested the sometimes elasticated evidence the two detectives had. But his only real purpose here was to report back to Jimmy Doyle.

Using the carrot and stick method the two detectives slowly and methodically had worn them down. In the end, with threats of long prison sentences, they had both coughed up. As had been suspected it had been Jimmy Doyle who had made the bomb and was the person who had ordered them to plant it on Roy Coombs' boat.

It was now time to put the last pieces of the jigsaw in place; the final stages of Operation Ghost. It was three thirty on Wednesday afternoon when DCI Collins, his sergeant and two other detectives drove to the National Crime Agencies nondescript offices on a nearby trading estate. Their purpose now was to execute the arrests of four men.

Jimmy Doyle would be apprehended that evening by DCI Collins and his team. The NCA would arrest Duncan Hicks and Sahil Ali early the next morning upon their release at Winson Green prison. Warren Turner would also be apprehended at his home by a separate team the same morning.

Following a final briefing the DCI and his team departed the NCA office at six o'clock for the drive across Birmingham City. Previously unbeknown to them at twenty minutes past five, a passer-by had rung the fire service to report smoke coming out of a window at the Blue Diamond Club. By the time the three fire appliances reached the scene the building, as predicted by Jimmy Doyle, was an inferno. When DCI Collins and his team arrived, all they could do was stand and watch as the fire fighters battled the blaze.

The sergeant asked, 'Do you reckon Doyle's inside Guv?'

DCI Collins smiled. 'No such luck. He's too bloody cunning for that. Whatever rabbit hole he's gone down, I doubt he will emerge for some time.'

A damp grey dawn broke over Winson Green prison. Duncan Hicks and Sahil Ali took one last look at the small cells in which they had been incarcerated for the last two years. At eight o'clock precisely, the heavy steel gates would open and they would step back into freedom.

Their associates had been eagerly awaiting this day, so they and their two bosses could once again return to their criminal activities. Unbeknown to Hicks and Ali, they would be the only two people exiting the gates that morning. At the request of the NCA, other inmates due for release would be held back by one hour.

At the same time as the scheduled release of Hicks and Ali, the bookie, Peter Baxter, Indian restaurant owner, Amit Thakur, and publican, Gerry Carter met at the greasy spoon café in Sparkbrook. As they brooded over mugs of stewed tea there was no such elation at the prospect of the release of their tormenters.

Amit Thakur asked, 'So have you heard anymore from this detective about the Roy Coombs file?'

Despondently Peter Baxter replied, 'I did speak to him recently, and again he said it was part of a larger investigation.'

Gerry Carter laughed. 'Exactly, they're not interested in us. They have bigger fish to fry.'

Peter sighed. His two friends had trusted him and he had let them down.

Two unmarked white National Crime Agency vans, both with blacked out windows, pulled up outside Winson Green prison. Each van parked either side of the short approach road, facing the gates. An unmarked car containing armed officers parked directly opposite affording them a clear view.

It had been expected that some of Hicks and Ali's people would be there to meet them. Knowing their reputation for violence no chances were being taken. One of the officers in the unmarked car nudged his partner. A black BMW had arrived and parked a short distance from the prison entrance.

The digital clock on their police car dashboard showed it was fifteen minutes before the gates opened. Two men got out of the BMW, lit cigarettes and sat on the bonnet. As the minutes ticked down the NCA men in the vans strapped on stab vests.

In a stubby, square tower to one side of the high walls a clock struck eight. Slowly the reinforced steel portal slid open. Hicks and Ali blinked as the bright morning sun caught their eyes. They stepped forward, breathing in the fresh air. The gates slid closed behind them. There was a shout from the two men leaning on the BMW. Hicks waved. They both moved towards the car.

Suddenly the van doors flew open. Hicks and Ali were surrounded by six NCA officers. One of the men from the BMW went for his inside pocket. The armed officers leapt from their car aiming their multi calibre rifles at the two men. They shouted, 'Armed police! Lay face down on the floor! Do it now!'

Few words were spoken before Hicks and Ali were placed in separate vans and driven away, their hopes of freedom a distant dream.

In Edgbaston, an affluent area of Birmingham, an unmarked car pulled up outside a smart detached house. Apart from the occasional passing car and the postman delivering letters it was quiet in the tree lined street. Behind the mock Tudor style façade Detective Superintendent Turner had just showered and was dressing in one of his expensive suits. His unsuspecting wife was in the kitchen giving their two young children breakfast.

The knock was loud and purposeful. DSU Turner opened the door to be confronted by two NCA officers. After a brief discussion they stepped inside. Twenty minutes later Turner, his hands cuffed behind his back, was escorted down the drive and into the rear of the waiting car. On the doorstep his tearful wife watched as their comfortable lifestyle disintegrated before her eyes.

Later that morning in the police station, DCI Collins kicked the coffee machine again then walked casually back to his office. Sitting at his desk he sipped the muddy beverage and waited for the call. It came at midday. His female colleague at the NCA said with her customary bluntness. 'It's done.'

Lying back in his chair he smiled. Now he could retire a happy man. But there was one more thing he had to do. Picking up the phone he called Peter Baxter. After relaying the news of the arrests to the much relieved bookie, he said, 'There's someone I'd like you to meet. Can you come into the station this afternoon?'

Behind the police station was a sixties built brick building consisting of five floors. This was the section house where newly appointed, or single officers, could live. After meeting Peter Baxter outside the station, the DCI took him to the fourth floor of the block. Before unlocking the door to one of the flats, the DCI asked, 'Do you believe in ghosts?'

Peter laughed. 'No. Nor aliens.'

In the sitting room a man in his early sixties was watching horse racing on the television.

'Mr Coombs,' said DCI Collins. 'I believe you two know each other.'

He stood up smiling, 'Indeed we do. Hello Peter.'

PREVIOUS BOOKS BY THE AUTHOR

The Stowaway series:
The Stowaway
The Golden Windlass
The Strangers
The Breaking Point
Time and Tide

Other titles:
One Paddle Short of a Lock
The Cards you're Dealt
Pecked Bread and Fallen Leaves: a collection of poetry

Printed in Dunstable, United Kingdom

72413176R00121